"It's jus _____ **hen they ca** _____

"Are you sure?" Suddenly—shockingly—Luke wasn't sure himself.

"Extremely. Lust is just a bodily function, right? So…we deal with it."

"Are you trying to say we *should* have sex?" he asked, incredulous.

"Well, not here," Faith said. They were in a storage closet. At the clinic. With patients just down the hall. "But after work. Just on the Saturdays you're still honor bound to give me."

"What about after that?"

"Well, you'd just have to let me go. I'm sorry, Luke, but like we said, we're just too different."

Luke should've been doing the happy dance. But he didn't feel like dancing. "Faith, you deserve more than that."

"It's what I want." She arched, letting her tight, hot nipples rub against his chest. "Are you going to turn me down, Luke?"

The thought made him want to cry. "No. Definitely, no…"

Dear Reader,

I think a bigger-than-life hero is fun to read about—there's something so inherently sexy about him. I'm hoping you think so, too, as Dr. Luke Walker is both bigger than life and extremely sexy. He's certainly sure of himself...maybe more than any other hero I've ever written. He's a black-and-white kind of guy—no middle ground for our Dr. Luke. So it was fun letting Faith McDowell have her way with him and show him all that gray in between.

And getting to do this miniseries with Lori Foster (*Riley*, June 2003, Temptation #930) and Donna Kauffman (*Sean*, July 2003, Temptation #934)...talk about exciting! I hope you enjoy our AMERICAN HEROES, readers!

Happy reading,

Jill Shalvis

P.S. Be sure to visit me at my Web site, www.jillshalvis.com.

Books by Jill Shalvis

JILL SHALVIS

LUKE

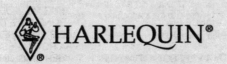

HARLEQUIN®

TORONTO • NEW YORK • LONDON
AMSTERDAM • PARIS • SYDNEY • HAMBURG
STOCKHOLM • ATHENS • TOKYO • MILAN • MADRID
PRAGUE • WARSAW • BUDAPEST • AUCKLAND

To Lori Foster and Donna Kauffman,
for graciously sharing their readers with me.

ISBN 0-373-69138-6

LUKE

Copyright © 2003 by Jill Shalvis.

1

THE TWO NEARLY NAKED WOMEN frolicked in the waves only yards away and Luke Walker yawned. *Yawned*.

Oh, definitely, he was on the edge of burnout. On the edge and skating on thin ground. Behind him stood his home on the Malibu bluffs. In front of him were the bikini babes.

And inside him...exhaustion. Actually, he was far beyond exhaustion and heading straight for brain dead, but who was keeping track?

Unfortunately, even sleep couldn't help him, not today, not when every time he closed his eyes, he transported himself back.

Blood soaking his hands, splattering across his scrubs as he knelt on the moving gurney next to the far-too-still six-year-old boy. Orderlies racing them down the hallway towards surgery as Luke barked orders, held the boy's wound shut and prayed to a God he wasn't sure could hear him.

"So why aren't you down there frolicking with the babes?"

At the heavily Spanish accented voice, Luke groaned and opened his eyes. Carmen DeCosta took great pleasure in thinking she knew him well enough to boss him around. She stood there with her hands on her ample hips, waiting for an answer.

Was everyone going to give him that bug-on-a-slide look today? "Don't go there," he warned. "I'm trying to take a breather here."

"Good. You don't do that enough." With a spryness that belied her chunkiness, the dark-haired, dark-skinned—or should he say *thick*-skinned—woman dropped to the sand next to him, apparently taking a break from her duties cleaning his house to offer him her opinions on his life. Nothing new. She liked to boss him around. She liked to fuss over him as well, and he knew she thought of herself as a surrogate mother since his own was gone.

But he didn't need one. Actually, he'd never needed one. And yet somehow he'd never managed to convince her of that.

He looked out at the pounding surf, at the ridiculous bikinied beach babes, and saw nothing but Dr. Leo Atkinson from South Village Medical Center frowning at him. Luke was head of the E.R., but Leo was head of surgery. He was also director of all the various department heads. So while technically they were peers, Leo, sitting on the hospital board and also town council, had far more power. Which was fine with Luke, who just wanted to be left alone to heal people, not navigate the bullshit, ass-kissing waters that was hospital politics.

You went too far, Luke, Leo had said. *You're a marketing nightmare, and now, unfortunately, something has to be done or you won't be named E.R. Head again in this century.*

He was referring, of course, to when Luke had let out a statement regarding the idiocracy of the bureaucrats running their hospital after he'd learned they'd helped fund Healing Waters Clinic, a place where conventional medicine wasn't even practiced.

The comment had been leaked to the press, who'd gleefully reported it in the *Los Angeles Times* and *The South Village Press,* among others. The fallout had been immediate. The owner of the clinic had called the hospital board, who'd gone to Leo, who'd gone to Luke.

Fix it. Retract the statement.

Not that easy. To Luke things were black and white. Give him a medical emergency and he could either fix it or not. Mostly he could.

No gray areas, no middle ground.

But Healing Waters Clinic... They worked in that gray area with aromatherapy, massage therapy, acupressure...*yoga.*

That the board funded such a place when the hospital turned away patients who couldn't pay, patients who legitimately needed their help, was asinine.

In his humble opinion.

Which wasn't so humble, apparently. He was going to be punished for his outburst. In the worst way possible.

"It's just the way it is," Leo had said in only slight apology. "You're amazing with your patients, but when it comes to everyone else—the board, your staff, *everyone*—they say you're a nightmare, and even I have to agree. You've got to learn to soften your approach, Luke, or good as you are, you're going to get your walking papers. In light of that, you're going to volunteer your services at the Healing Waters Clinic every Saturday for three months."

Luke had stared at him for one full moment. "Why don't you just take away my license," he'd finally said. "It would be less painful."

Leo had laughed over that, then slapped him on the back. "Enjoy it, Luke. This is your last chance to prove you're a team player."

A team player. Woo hoo, his biggest goal. *Not.* He glowered at the ocean, brooding.

"Nice view." Carmen nodded to the bikini crowd.

He shrugged. Damn it, he was a good doctor. A great doctor. That should be all that mattered, not how well he could spin a tale for the press, or appease the people around him.

"So..." Carmen leaned back on her elbows, looking

as if she didn't plan on more cleaning anytime soon. "How many patients did you see today?"

Luke sighed. "A lot."

"Any interesting *female* patients? Say...someone interesting enough to date?"

Why was it a single man was always such an irresistible setup? "Why?"

"Because one of them left you some cookies. Must have made a huge impression on her, Dr. Luke."

One big wave after another hit the shore, causing shrieks of joy from the bathing beauties. Luke inhaled the salt air, then slowly let it out.

"Don't you want to know who left the cookies? Let me help you remember. Blond, tall, gorgeous. And..." Carmen cupped her hands out in front of her chest. "Stacked."

Inhaling more salt air...

"Are you listening?"

"I'm trying not to."

"Oh, you. Do you know who left the cookies or not?"

Lucy Cosine. He'd stitched her up earlier in the week when she'd neglected to stop at a red light and had plowed into a mail truck, putting her head through her windshield. She was late twenties, rich, husband-searching based on status (her words, not his) and apparently Luke fit the bill.

Too bad he wasn't on the market. "Are the cookies any good?"

"Bah." Carmen made a face. "Mine are better." In front of them, one of the two women went down under a wave and came up laughing like an idiot. "Tough job you got there, doctor. Hard to believe you can't manage to find yourself a woman." She looked him over critically. "Maybe you have a problem with your attention span?"

Luke studied the sharp, blue sky, amazingly void of Southern California smog today. "Funny."

"Love is a good stress reliever, you know."

"We are absolutely not going to discuss sex."

"I said *love*. Not sex." Carmen's voice was filled with mischief. "But sex works too."

A rough laugh escaped Luke at that. Always, no matter how bad things got—and they'd been pretty bad here and there—Carmen could somehow provide the comic relief. "You're ruining my bad mood for me."

"Good." Carmen beamed, and reaching over, she noisily kissed his cheek. "I just want you to be happy, Luke. Everyone deserves a little happiness."

"I am." Or he had been happy enough anyway, until Leo's ultimatum today.

"Nah, you need a woman for that, one to share your

heart, your home, your bed, and not necessarily in that order.''

Luke would take the woman in his bed part, just about any night of the week—if he had the time and wasn't on call—but a woman in his heart? Not a chance in hell, not when he lived and breathed his work. What woman in her right mind would want a man who didn't have anything left to give?

And what woman in her right mind would want a man, a doctor, who'd just been slapped with a disciplinary action that was likely going to kill him?

Working in a natural healing clinic for God's sake. For three months. Unbelievable.

Truly, he couldn't think of a worse fate.

WHEN HER HOROSCOPE SAID the stars weren't aligned in her favor, Faith McDowell should have believed it and pulled the covers back over her head.

But lounging in bed had never been her style. As to what was her style, she hadn't quite figured that out yet. She didn't have much time for that.

On autopilot, she turned on the shower, cranked up the radio, and lit a jasmine candle guaranteed to uplift and stimulate.

Soaping up, she sang at the top of her lungs, because singing was an excellent energy releaser. It worked for all of sixty seconds, which was how long it took for her brain to refuse to be sidetracked by music and scents, and face reality.

Her reality wasn't easy to face.

Just this week, she'd had to give herself a pay cut as Director of Healing Waters Clinic. That meant a lot of macaroni and cheese in her immediate future.

But at least she still had a clinic, and a lovely building in South Village to house it. She'd opened the place last year, right on North Union Street, the main drag of the town that rivaled Sunset Strip in pedestrian traffic. She'd opened it after four years of being a nurse practitioner.

Working in a San Diego E.R. she'd seen it all, every kind of suffering, and had always felt modern medicine wasn't doing all it could. But no one had wanted to hear her ideas of natural healing, of homeopathic healing, of all the ancient and established methods that really worked, not when there were multiple gunshot wounds, motor vehicle accident injuries and other emergency traumas to deal with every day.

Here, in her healing clinic, she could concentrate on those ideas considered outside the lines of conventional medicine, she could finally concentrate on easing suffering in less invasive ways. Shockingly, the powers that be at the local hospital had been willing to refer people to her, and later had even helped fund her efforts, and she'd never been happier.

Until one of the local doctors, a Dr. Luke Walker, had publicly raised his nose at her work there. She'd faced such disdain before, only she'd underestimated Dr. Walker's reputation and following. Once the public had heard his opinion, once they'd realized she didn't have his support, she'd ended up spending a good part of her day answering questions and debating medical practices, which in turn meant more time with each patient, creating more backlog and long waits. As a result, people weren't coming back.

Mercifully, the hospital had stepped in, promising a quick fix. They were giving the clinic an extra hand, one that belonged to Dr. Walker himself, as a matter of fact, for three months of weekends. *There*, she thought, with her first smile of the day. A silver lining. So therefore, her horoscope had to be wrong.

She was so sure of it, that when she ran out of hot water with conditioner still in her hair, it was a shock. Then the bathroom scale decided *not* to be her friend, and to top it all off, she couldn't find clean socks.

Already wary of the day and it wasn't even seven o'clock. She went downstairs. There was one negative thing about living over the clinic on a major street in a major town filled with people who got up early. The street was already filled with joggers, bicyclists, early shoppers and workers; the majority of them young, hip, urban, and far better put together than she had ever been at seven in the morning.

She located her newspaper, which hadn't made it to the stoop, but had instead landed in the small patch of wet grass. Picking it up with two fingers, the soggy, chewed mess fell apart like confetti. With a sigh, she looked up into the face of her neighbor's eighty-pound Doberman. "Again, Tootsie?"

Tootsie lifted his chin and gave her a doggie smile before trotting off.

"That's what you get for living at your work." This from Shelby Anderson, her co-naturopathic practitioner at Healing Waters, and Faith's best friend. She came up the walkway and followed Faith into the back door of the clinic, looking more like an actress in her flowered scrubs than the real thing.

Faith knew Shelby couldn't help the fact that her blond hair was always just right, and that she needed hardly any makeup to glow, or that her long, willowy body was the only one on the planet that scrubs actually looked good on, but it was still a little irksome, especially so early in the morning.

"I live above my work, not *at* my work," Faith corrected, tugging at her scrubs, which most definitely were not nearly as flattering on her as they were on Shelby.

"Above work, at work, same thing," Shelby said. "Both suck."

Faith looked down at her chewed newspaper. "Okay, sometimes, yes."

Shelby set down her purse and leaned against the counter, sipping at the herbal tea she'd brought. "Would you like some? You look beat already."

"Gee, and I thought I'd used my makeup concealer correctly."

Shelby smiled. "You don't wear any makeup, much less concealer, so stop it. Just remember, every time you let yourself run down, you get the flu."

Complete with exhaustion, sweaty shakes and a killer headache. She'd been plagued by a pesky tropical virus for years, more so lately, since she'd opened the clinic, but she didn't intend to let it get her again.

She'd caught the virus in Bora-Bora years ago while there as a child with her missionary parents, and ever since she'd been susceptible to it. She'd been extra careful, getting rest, eating right—not difficult since she loved food—and for the most part ate extremely healthy. If one didn't count her secret and shameful chocolate addiction.

Oh, wait, she'd given up chocolate. Really. And not because her mother had a tendency to be chunky and Faith was afraid of getting the same way, but because she wanted to practice what she preached. She wanted to live a healthy life.

Her body just didn't always agree with her. "I'm fine," she told Shelby.

"Why don't you do an herbal treatment today? Or better yet, let me do it for you?"

"Maybe." She needed to get the clinic back on track first. It shouldn't take too much. For the most part, the clinic itself was successful. People loved the services they offered. The problem was that most insurance plans didn't cover those services, so she was forced to charge far less than she should. As a result, she was understaffed, and didn't have the budget to hire more people.

The good news... Dr. Walker's services were going to be free. For three months.

"Do you really think Dr. Walker is going to help us?"

"Yes, and before you ask...he's late. I know."

Shelby looked at her watch again. "Twenty bucks says he's not going to show."

He'd better—the hospital had promised he'd be here with bells on, and a smile to boot, doing his best to give support and reverse any publicity damage he'd caused.

Faith was counting on it. Dr. Luke Walker was extremely well respected in the community. People listened to him. With any luck, he'd be far kinder to the clinic once he'd seen them in action, and he'd spread the word. "He'll show."

"Okay, but only a few minutes until patients arrive, and if he's not here..."

"I know, I know." Back-Up City, with patients grumbling, complaining, *leaving*...something she couldn't let happen.

Still, they waited fruitlessly for him for thirty minutes, and when they were indeed backing up, getting behind schedule, Shelby and Faith again met in the hallway with twin worried expressions.

"It is his usual day off," Faith said. "Maybe he's sleeping in by accident."

"Then we're screwed."

"No we're not." Nothing if not determined, she grabbed her keys. "Tell me we have his address."

"It's on your desk." Shelby smiled. "Going to haul him out of bed?"

"If need be. I know we're already so backed up, but if I get another practitioner in the house, it'll be worth me leaving for a little while." Faith chewed her lip. "Better wish me luck."

"Oh yeah, I'll wish you luck. You're going to need it."

FAITH STOOD OUTSIDE Dr. Luke Walker's house on the coast and knocked again. When no one answered, she checked the address against the piece of paper she held. It had to be right. The house was a block-and-glass palace fit for a prestigious doctor, as was the forest-green Jaguar in the driveway.

She glanced at her late-eighties Ford Escort and sighed. She wasn't a confrontational person by nature despite her innate stubbornness and her fondness for being right. Truth was, in a fight she figured she'd roll over like a puppy and show her belly. But with her clinic's destiny at stake, she felt like a protective momma bear.

Make that a mountain lioness, and her claws were out.

The curse of the redheaded temperament, she supposed, and self-consciously patted her long, red—and unruly—hair. Well, tough. He'd asked for her temper by being late. He had a duty, this Saturday and every Saturday for the next three months, to her and the clinic.

She knocked again, louder now. Waited with what she thought was admirable patience. And started tapping her foot when no one answered. She glanced back at the car that assured her someone was indeed home.

And knocked yet again, listening with some satisfaction to the echo of her pounding as it reverberated through the house.

Sleeping, was he? Damn the man, snoozing bliss-fully while her life went down the tubes—

Then the door whipped open, and suddenly she was staring right at a man's bare chest. Tilting her head up, and up, she found her Dr. Luke Walker, and swallowed hard.

She'd heard about him, of course, in the occasional article in the newspaper, especially once he'd made his infamous comments about her clinic. But Dr. Luke Walker in the flesh was like nothing she'd ever expe-rienced. He was leaner, harder than she'd expected, the lines of his face more stark, his nearly naked body far tougher than she would have imagined.

"Yes?" His vivid blue eyes had landed right on her, and for some odd reason she couldn't find her tongue much less form a sentence.

His dark, slightly wavy hair was short and bed-ruffled, his mouth grim. At her silence, a muscle in his cheek ticked.

Oh, and he wore nothing but low-slung sweatpants that he hadn't bothered to tie.

Bad attitude personified, all one hundred eighty pounds of him.

Clearly, she'd indeed gotten him out of bed, and yet there was nothing even halfway sleepy about his sear-ing gaze as it swept over her. "Who are you and why are you trying to knock my door down?"

"Faith McDowell," she said, trying really hard not to notice all his corded muscles and sinews, all his smooth, tanned skin. For some reason the sight of him, up close and personal and practically naked, made her feel a little insecure.

"Well, Faith McDowell, what do you want?"

"I..." What did she want? Oh, yes, her clinic, her *life*. Her lioness claws came back out. "I came to drive you to the clinic, because clearly, your car isn't working, which would explain why you didn't show up at the clinic an hour ago when you were supposed to."

He just looked at her.

She tried valiantly not to look at her watch or rush him along. "We have patients scheduled for you, remember?" *Tell me you remember.*

"I remember." He said this in a voice that assured her going to the clinic was the last thing he wanted to do, right after, say, having a fingernail slowly pulled out. "I just wish I didn't."

"So...your alarm neglected to go off?" This time she didn't hold herself back and purposely glanced at her watch. And then nearly panicked at the time.

"It isn't time for it to go off."

"Right, because as a doctor, you can breeze into the clinic more than an hour *after* it's opened, with no concern for how that would throw off our schedule." How could she have forgotten the arrogant God complex of doctors? "Look, I'm sorry you don't want to do this, but we have a full load of patients today. Thanks to your tardiness, we're already far behind. The longer I stand here waiting for you, the worse it's going to get."

"My *tardiness?*"

"If we get much more behind before lunch, trust me, it's not going to be pretty."

He ran a hand over his jaw, and the dark shadow there rasped in the morning silence. "I was told 9:00 a.m."

"*Seven.*"

"That's not what I was told."

A misunderstanding then. Fine. Annoying, but they could get past this. "I'm sorry, but you were told wrong."

He scratched his chest, the one she was trying not to gape at. Obviously, he did something other than treat patients all day long because that body of his was well-kept, without a single, solitary inch of excess.

"I wouldn't have agreed to seven," he said. "Seven is too early."

"Well, for three months' worth of weekends, get used to it." Surely, it had to be against the law to be so mouth-wateringly gorgeous and such an insensitive jerk at the same time. It was his fault he was in this spot. People were waiting for him right this very second, though she imagined that was the story of his life. Dr. Luke Walker had been born to heal, or so legend claimed at South Village Medical Center, one of the busiest hospitals in all of Southern California. His hands held and delivered miracles every single day. His patients worshipped him because of it.

The people who worked with him; the other doctors, nurses, staff—everyone understood and respected that extraordinary gift, but according to gossip—and there was never a shortage of that in her field—there weren't many who held a great love for him personally. Faith knew much of that was simple pettiness and jealousy. After all, he was only thirty-five, and the rumors predicted he'd be running the hospital by the time he hit forty.

If they could fix his habit of speaking his mind, that is.

Because while he was astonishingly compassionate and giving and tender with his patients, he did not generally extend those people skills to anyone else, such as the people he worked with. Faith had heard the stories and figured he didn't mean to be so gruff and hurried and impatient, he just didn't suffer fools well.

But now, she had to wonder if maybe he was just missing the be-nice-to-people gene. "I realize this isn't important to you, working at the clinic, but you promised."

He let out a rough sound that managed to perfectly convey his annoyance, and for Faith, it was the last straw.

"And really, this is your own fault anyway," she pointed out. "If you hadn't made that statement that got out to the press saying you thought our clinic was worthless, you wouldn't be stuck paying penance for three months' worth of Saturdays. You could be out golfing—"

"Golfing?" His eyes widened incredulously. *"Golfing—"*

"Or whatever it is you rich doctors do with all the money you make off your patients."

"My God, you have a mouth on you."

Yes. Yes, she did. It had gotten her into trouble plenty of times, but damn it, this was important to her.

Still, what was it her mother had said... You could catch more flies with honey? With a sigh, she swallowed her pride. "I'm...sorry." Not words she used often. "It's just that we really need you."

With his arms crossed over that bare chest, and a frown still masking his chiseled-in-stone face, he looked far more like a thug than a doctor. A beautiful thug, but still a dangerous, edgy one. He let out a disparaging noise, shoved his fingers through his dark hair, making it stick up all the more. "I'd like to get one thing straight here. I never said the clinic was worthless. What I said was I didn't understand why the hospital gave your clinic money when—" He took in her humor-the-jerk expression and broke off. "Okay, forget it. I'll be there soon."

"I'll just wait and drive you."

"That's not necessary."

"I think it is."

"Why? Is there an emergency waiting for me right now?"

"Uh..."

"Are *you* in need of medical attention of any kind?"

"Well, no, but—"

"Then I'll be there. On my own. Soon." He actually turned to go inside the house, dismissing her.

Without stopping to think—a personality disorder she'd been saddled with since childhood—Faith slapped a hand on his front door and held it open. "I'd really rather wait for you."

Still turned away, Dr. Walker let out a long-suffering sigh, which brought her attention upward past the sleek, powerful flesh and sinew of his back to the widest, most tension-filled shoulders she'd ever seen.

Unfortunately, he turned then, and caught her in the act of ogling him. Not a word came out of his mouth, but no words were necessary, not when his highly vexed expression did all his talking for him.

She cleared her throat and tried to ignore the blush that crept over her face. Another redheaded curse. "You do understand the clinic's already full—"

"Yeah." He closed his eyes, then lifted his hands to his temples. The untied sweatpants shifted down an inch or so on his hips, revealing more flat belly.

A hot flash raced through her body. That pesky tropical virus again. It had to be.

"I don't get it." He sounded baffled. "Why do you even want me there? You know I'm into conventional, modern medicine. The good, old-fashioned, scientific stuff. So—"

"Actually, the alternative means of medicine that we use is the good, old-fashioned way, thousands of years old in some cases. So really, your 'conventional' medicine, at only a couple hundred years old, is the baby."

His jaw ticked again. "I still don't see what massage therapy, aromatherapy, acupressure, yoga and herbs have to do with me."

"The alternative practices can be blended in with the more conventional ones, and with that, we can offer people something more. Something better."

"But I don't know how to treat people that way."

"It's just a way of life," she said. "You'll have plenty

to offer. Mostly credibility at first, but..." She broke off when he put his hands on his hips.

Her gaze glued itself to his loose sweat bottoms, her breath blocking in her throat. If they slipped just another fraction of an inch or so—

"Look, I had a really long night." His weary tone drew her eyes back up to his exhausted ones. "And I thought I had an extra few hours. I'll hurry, but I don't need an audience, so if you don't mind—"

"Well actually, I—"

The door shut in her face.

2

CARMEN SHOWED UP IN LUKE'S inside hallway, having clearly just let herself in the back door. She blocked his path to the stairs with that look on her face that told him he was getting no peace until she spoke her mind.

"Gee," she said. "Hard to imagine how a man with all your charm could still be single."

Ignoring her, he headed wearily up the stairs. He'd been up all night, shifting through nightmares that forced him to relive losing six-year-old Johnny Garcia to the war zone that had become Los Angeles. "Just wake me in ten minutes, okay?" If he could catch a few more minutes, he'd be okay. He'd be human. He'd be able to remember that on most days he loved this life, loved what he did for a living.

"She was a sweet girl," Carmen said, disgusted. "Coming to pick you up. And you chased her off."

"She was a woman, not a girl."

"So you did notice."

Yeah, he'd noticed. Faith McDowell's sexy softness contrasted with her cool voice and clear green eyes, and any red-blooded male would have noticed. She had long, curly hair the color of a fiery sunset and had worn a pair of scrubs decorated with smiley faces covered by a lightweight, open sweater that hugged her body, showing off creamy skin and lush curves. Disgusted with himself, Luke put a hand on the wood banister and started climbing.

He'd definitely been too long without sex if scrubs with smiley faces had turned him on.

But now, if he was very lucky, he could close his eyes for a few more minutes. Sleep was far more important than sex these days. Then he'd shower, grab some steaming, black coffee, and maybe, just maybe, feel sane again.

"How are you supposed to start a family someday if you chase off all the women?" Carmen called up the stairs. "Answer me *that*."

He answered *that* with one concise muttered word.

Carmen tsked. "You were rude, and isn't she your boss at the clinic?"

Yeah, and just what he needed, yet another politically correct bureaucrat telling him what to do. And yet... Maybe Carmen had a point. If he tried harder, added a smile, even turned on the charm he used to relax his patients...he might actually get his sentence reduced.

Luke pictured the woman's wild, gloriously red hair bouncing in the morning sea breeze. The sparks in her eyes. He thought of the way she'd drawn in a huge deep breath just before she'd blasted him, as if she was so amazingly angry she could hardly think.

Nope. He doubted he could get her to reduce his "volunteer" time. She wanted his head on a platter—her platter. He'd written his own death sentence, damn it.

The doorbell rang.

"Ah, hell, what now?" He looked down at Carmen. "I've had five hours sleep in two days."

Carmen's entire face softened. "Yes, baby. You work too hard."

"I just need a few more minutes of shut-eye. You can chase her off, okay?"

"What if it's an emergency?"

"It's not. It's just Red, looking to take a piece out of my hide for being late."

Carmen grinned. "She did seem to be a natural, temperamental redhead, didn't she? You know, rumor has it you used to be able to soothe a woman. They say you even used to *like* women."

He still did. In bed. But right now he was too tired to think of sharing his mattress, plus he doubted Faith McDowell would be interested anyway. She seemed to expect more out of a person than what he had in mind.

He didn't have more. He gave it all to work and his

patients, gave everything he had so that at the end of the day, there wasn't anything left.

Maybe it was the way he'd been raised, with parents who'd rarely taken the time for him or his brother, Matt, pawning them off like unwanted luggage on everyone and anyone who'd take them. Maybe it was because it'd been so long since he'd taken a breather, he could hardly remember who he really was. He didn't care.

He wanted sleep.

The doorbell rang again.

"Tell her I'll be there soon."

"Clearly, she needs you now."

With a groan, he padded back down the stairs, glaring at Carmen, who unlike everyone else in his life, didn't back down from him. "This is why I hired you, you know. You're supposed to scare people away."

"Stop being so curmudgeonly."

Stopping in midstride, he stared at her. *"Curmudgeonly?"*

"It's someone who's grumpy, and—"

"I know what it means, and I'm not— Oh, forget it." He settled his hand on the knob and hauled it open, finding himself looking down into the intelligent, and still fuming, eyes of the woman who was to be his boss at the clinic for the next three months' worth of Saturdays.

You used to like women.

Oh, but he definitely still did. He just wasn't used to being looked at as if he was pond scum, especially by a wildly attractive woman with steam coming out of her ears.

Absolutely too long without sex.

"You're still not ready," she said exasperated.

Deciding there should be a law against facing a furious woman before having a cup of coffee, no matter how lovely she was, he shook his head. The question was, would he ever be ready for a day full of aromatherapy and yoga? God save him. Despite his to-the-bone-fatigue, his lips quirked. "I need more than sixty seconds."

Her gaze appeared to be riveted on his chest. "We don't have more than sixty seconds," she murmured.

He'd stumbled half-naked out of bed to get the door earlier, and now, given the way she looked at him, he glanced down to make sure his sweats covered all the essentials. Yes, he was covered, but if she kept staring at him like that, as if he was a long, tall glass of water and she was dying of thirst, those essentials were going to make themselves known regardless of his irritation.

"Here." Carmen materialized from behind him and wisely shoved a steaming cup of coffee in his hands. He nearly cried in gratitude, and might have actually hugged her, but then she said to Faith McDowell in apology, "Give him until the coffee's gone. Two minutes tops, he'll be human again. I promise."

"Oh." Faith smiled sweetly. At Carmen, not Luke. "Yes, I understand. Thank you." Kindness and genuine caring poured from her. Her voice, light now that it was directed at someone other than him, was the most amazingly sweet, musical voice Luke had ever heard.

It reminded him of...sex. Unbelievable, what sleep deprivation could do to a man.

Carmen and Red—her hair was whipping around her shoulders, long and wild—watched him with twin expressions of expectation, waiting for his coffee to work the miracle that wasn't going to happen, not today. "I'm going upstairs now," he said carefully. "To get showered and dressed."

"Is that going to take more than five minutes?" His new boss glanced at her watch, quivering with impatience.

"Ten," he said, then paused as if he really cared what she thought. "Is that okay?"

She considered this. Considered him. "Just remember, the patients are counting on you." Her voice was cool again. The wind picked up, and with a sound of annoyance, she tossed back her wild hair. Her sweater, thin and ineffective against the chill, slipped off one shoulder, revealing the fact she was...chilly.

In an odd reaction, considering he didn't like her, Luke felt a physical stirring at the sight.

Sleep deprived, he reminded himself. A dangerous thing.

Shrugging back into the sweater, Faith crossed her arms over her chest. "This is really a two-way street, you know. I'll be helping you, too."

"How, exactly, is that possible?"

"You'll be practicing—and hopefully improving—your people skills."

It was one thing to be so tired as to be lusting after a woman who thought him an insensitive idiot, but it was another thing entirely to let her think he *needed* her in any way. He needed no one, and he certainly didn't need help with his people skills.

"You might not realize this, but one of the basic people skills is charm. I can help you there."

Carmen laughed at that, but when he whipped around with a murderous expression, she vanished into the kitchen.

"In order to charm," Faith said. "You need to stimulate the people around you. Can you do that?"

He thought of the inexplicable way his body had reacted to her. "Stimulation isn't a problem," he managed with a straight face.

"Good, because this is *very* important. The clinic is very important, and we have so much to do. Today alone we have babies to deliver, allergies and sinus infections, healing bones and…"

Luke's mind drifted back to her body. How was it she looked so good in those scrubs? But she did, she looked soft and curvy, and—

"Dr. Walker?" Hands on her hips, she cocked her head. "Are you still listening to me?"

Oh yeah. "Stimulate."

Looking suddenly a bit wary, she backed out of his house.

Yeah, Red, I advise you to run like hell.

"Well, I'll let you get on with getting ready.…" She bit her lip as once more she ran her gaze down his body.

And this time, his body definitely reacted.

She took another few steps, backing down his porch now. "I'll…uh…be waiting."

It should have really ticked him off, but suddenly, that threat seemed far more like a promise. "Okay then," he said, and wondered why maybe, just maybe, he'd be looking forward to it.

FAITH DROVE AROUND THE back of Healing Waters Clinic and parked, then glanced in her rearview mirror.

Yep, Dr. Luke Walker was still following her in his fancy car that screamed success. She'd heard so much about him before this morning, but no one, not a single soul, not a single article, had ever mentioned his see-through light blue eyes, his fiery expression, the incredible, drool-inducing body that brought to mind far too many things that had nothing, nothing at all, to do with doctoring.

Grabbing her purse, she took a quick moment to inhale a long, calming breath. She was an expert in long, calming breaths, and yet the technique utterly and completely failed her now.

Hell of a time to give up chocolate, as she could use it now. A vicious craving for the secret stash of almond Hershey Kisses in her glove box overcame her. Just one, she thought, and nearly reached for them....

But she heard his door shut and hastily straightened, getting out of her car to greet him with a cool, distant smile on her face that absolutely had better hide her thoughts—her desperate need for that chocolate, her unthinkable, ridiculous attraction to him—because the bottom line was, beneath that amazing flesh and sinew, beneath his remarkable talent, beat the cold heart of a man who'd blindly put down her clinic to untold hundreds.

Her success was important to her. After all, everyone in her family succeeded. It was sort of a McDowell requirement. But more than that, she wanted this for all the people out there she was convinced she could help in a way conventional medicine couldn't.

And she wanted Luke to acknowledge that maybe, just maybe, he wasn't the only one who could make a difference in others' lives. She could too. And she'd prove it by showing him how invaluable the clinic could be.

Luke's own face was unsmiling as he moved toward her, but it wasn't even close to distant. He was still hot under the collar, and she had to say, the look was a good one on him. If one were to go for the dark, smoldering, attitude-ridden type of man.

Luckily, she didn't. She didn't go for any men—she didn't have time.

Together they turned to face her building. As with all the buildings in South Village, this one dated back to the early 1900s but had been well preserved. The two-story brick structure had once been a brewery, fully restored in the fifties. Thanks to her green thumb, it was surrounded by greenery, wildflowers and herbs she grew herself to use in her clinic. The sign hanging in front proudly read Healing Waters.

It was her baby, brainstormed during all those long, long nights of working insane hours as a nurse practitioner. The days when science and conventional medicine had been the only way. The right way. The days when her ideas of going deeper, healing more than just the body, but also the heart and soul had been mocked and grossly misunderstood in the hustling, bustling world of the E.R. she'd worked at in San Diego.

She'd prepared for this, she'd studied, gotten accredited in a variety of naturopathic areas. Now she could run diagnostic procedures, give vaccinations, assist in natural childbirth and even write limited prescriptions.

Yes, she still worked long, long hours, but these days the crazy hours actually left her satisfied and fulfilled because she was following her dream, healing people in ways conventional medicine had failed them.

But all Luke knew was that she was interrupting his weekends. "Ready?" she asked, and when he nodded, she led the way inside. The staff room was filled with organized clutter; everyone's personal belongings, files to be discussed, a small potted herbal garden she was babying along. As they walked through, she introduced him to any staff members they passed, while her mind raced ahead, trying to see the place as he would.

The waterfall in the reception area was on, the sound of the water cascading gently over a riverbed of rocks soothed the waiting patients, along with soft music she'd handpicked, the gentle lighting, and comfy ergonomic chairs. All in calming colors from the natural palette.

Definitely, deliberately, a world away from the E.R. Any E.R. "What do you think?"

"Well, no one is screaming in the waiting room," Luke said. "Always a good sign. Hmm, I suppose I can forgive the beaded curtains behind the receptionist. Who do you have on staff?"

He was a man used to being in charge of everything and everyone around him, she reminded herself. She couldn't fault that about him. He did have incredible skill, the reason she'd agreed to have him here in the first place. "Today we have two naturopathic practitioners, myself and Shelby Dodd, and also a massage therapist." But adding an M.D. on staff, one with Luke's prestige and incredible reputation, would surely boost her clientele.

And her checkbook. She hated to be so bottom-line about anything, but at the moment, hovering in the red, she had to be.

"Before we start," he said in a low voice, turning from his inspection of the place to look at her. "I just want you to know, I never said the clinic was worthless."

She stared up at his solemn features and nearly got lost in those light blue eyes. "The newspaper said—"

"They exaggerated." When she raised a brow, he sighed. "The hospital let twenty-five housekeeping employees go, employees who were forced to work four hours a week less than the full-time hours required for full benefits. The hospital insisted on that to save money, and then they let them go anyway, stating budget issues. The next day they sent your clinic a tidy sum."

"And you objected to that."

"Yes." His jaw went tight. "I objected to that."

She stared up into his face and felt an unexpected connection. "I would have objected, too," she said softly.

His eyes reflected surprise, but before he could say something, Shelby came around the corner and waved Faith down. "I just paged you. Woman in labor in room four. Fully dilated, fully effaced, freaking out, won't push, won't let us even take a peek anymore."

Faith set her purse down and started walking fast with Shelby at her side. "First baby?"

"Oh yeah. And she's a screamer."

"Get Guy—"

"He's already in there. If anyone can soothe a terrified pregnant lady..."

"Guy can." Guy Anders, their therapeutic massage therapist, had a voice that could sedate a gangbanger, and hands from heaven. He was their ace in the hole in situations like this, but still, as they rounded the corner and heard the screams, Faith cringed, both in sympathy for the woman and the people in the waiting room. "Dr. Walker—"

"I'll assist," he said from right behind her, and in fact, pushed into the room ahead of her.

Shelby lifted a brow, and Faith sighed. "He's used to being in charge."

Shelby let out a low laugh. "Well, since you are, too, this is going to be interesting."

They stepped into the room, where the screaming had stopped. Their patient, a woman in her midtwenties, lay in the bed, eyes huge on one Dr. Luke Walker, tall and leanly muscular, scrubbing his hands at the sink and talking to her the entire time. Then he hunkered down at her side, holding her hand, murmuring words too softly spoken for Faith to catch.

On the other side of the bed stood Guy, also tall and handsome, though unusually so with a purple stripe in his hair, and interesting tattoos and piercings. He shot Faith a bemused glance at being usurped, but didn't say a word.

Luke lifted his head and searched out Faith. "Margaret's ready to push now. I'm going to examine her first. Do you have a spare set of scrubs?"

"No!" Margaret sat straight up, not an easy feat with forty pounds of belly, and grabbed Luke by the collar. "No scrubbing, no changing! I want to push now!"

With her fists embedded in his shirt, Luke simply nodded calmly. "We can do that," he said in a soft, utterly authoritative yet kind voice, accepting gloves from Faith and snapping them on. To everyone he said, "I'll deliver in my street clothes."

Faith had just scrubbed and was already moving around to the foot of the bed. As a nurse practitioner she'd delivered more babies than she could count, simply because the doctors tended not to make it in time. Since she'd opened the clinic, there'd been hundreds more. Delivering babies was her favorite part of the job.

But Luke beat her to it. Leaning in, he murmured for her ears only, "She's obviously low pain tolerance, let's get her an epidural—"

"Her chart says she requested no drugs when she arrived."

He leaned in closer, stooping a little to stand eye-to-eye with her, and since they were eye-to-eye, she had no trouble seeing his carefully reined-in anger. "You don't believe in epidurals?"

"She requested to do this naturally," she repeated.

"Ah, the barbaric way then," he said. "Have you ever had a baby naturally, Faith McDowell?"

"No, and I'm fairly certain you haven't either. There

are plenty of other methods of easing pain—healing touch, herbs, imagery, pressure point therapy—"

"Let the patient decide against conventional pain meds," he said in a low, harsh whisper. "Let her decide in the moment, as in right now, not before she knows what she's getting into. And don't let your beliefs drive the decision, that's unfair."

"Fine." She shoved her chin in the air. "Clearly you have this situation under control. I'll tend to the other patients."

Without responding, he turned his attention to Margaret, his big body leaning over hers protectively, talking in that same low, gentle voice he'd never used on Faith.

She should be thankful for small favors, because that voice he didn't share with her made her tummy quiver and her legs feel funny. Boneless.

She really wished she'd had some chocolate.

MARGARET DELIVERED A beautiful eight-pound girl— without the epidural.

Faith delivered herself a pounding tension headache, the kind she'd had daily once upon a time, when she'd worked at the hospital.

"I need a new set of scrubs," Luke told her a couple of hours later on a rare two-minute break between patients.

"Fine." She strode down the hall, jerked open the supply closet and flipped on the light. She could smell him behind her, and one would think after hours of working with patients and running at a fast pace, he'd at least smell like it, but no. He smelled delicious, quite frankly. "How do you do that?" she asked grumpily.

"Do what?"

"Still smell good." She didn't point out how annoying that was. Or that her nose was straining to catch the scent of him.

"My mother always told me to smell good."

That startled a laugh out of her. "Really?"

"No." He was smiling. Good Lord, he shouldn't do that, because like his voice, it did funny things to her insides. "My mom didn't tell me anything," he said. "She had the nanny do it."

"Ah. Poor little rich boy, Dr. Walker?"

"Luke. And nah, not rich. My mother just didn't like messy things, and my brother and I were about as messy as they came."

No. No, she didn't want to hear this, that he was human, that he'd had a mother who hadn't mothered him, that he had a brother he'd obviously shared a lot with, that he...that he just might have had as lonely a childhood as she.

She found him a pair of scrubs, and as she pulled

them off the shelf, she fought back a laugh. Pink flow-ered scrubs. Smiling at the petty revenge, she turned around to hand them to him and found him much closer than she'd anticipated, as he'd stepped into the supply room behind her, craning his neck to check out the shelves. The last time she'd been this close to him, this morning, in fact, he'd been only half-dressed and tousled. Now his short, spiky dark hair had been combed, though his jaw still showed a shadow, prob-ably because she'd given him the bum's rush, not giv-ing him time to breathe, much less shave. It didn't change the potency of being this close to him. So close she could have leaned in a fraction of an inch and—

"Nicely stacked."

She watched his lips move, heard the words, and her jaw fell open as she looked down at the front of her scrubs, which so effectively hid her breasts. She had no idea how he'd—

"The shelves," he repeated slowly, frowning at her reaction. "They're nicely stocked. Organized."

Nicely stocked. *Stocked, you idiot.* Good God, she needed to get it together. This was *her* arena, her clinic, and lust, or whatever had happened to her genes and hormones since she'd set eyes on him, didn't have a place. Nope, no matter how big, bad and pulse-jerkingly magnificent the man standing close enough to grope was, she needed to ignore it all. "Um...thanks."

He'd complimented the clinic. Okay...maybe this *could* work, maybe they could find a happy medium—

"For a froufrou clinic," he added.

Nope. No happy medium.

3

FAITH DECIDED IT MUST be a full moon, as besides their
scheduled massage therapy, acupressure and aromatherapy appointments, they had an unusual number of women in labor, walk-ins and emergencies.

Either a full moon...or curiosity about Dr. Luke
Walker. She decided it didn't matter. She loved knowing people came to Healing Waters for help. She
ended up eating lunch on the run, which she hated to
do but it couldn't be helped. And by late afternoon,
she felt that familiar light-headedness—the one that
signaled her resistance was down—and still had that
monster headache that wouldn't quit.

If she didn't want to get sick, she needed a break,
horizontal on her couch in her office. And she'd get it,
she promised herself, as soon as she saw the seventeen-year-old waiting for her in room seven who
wanted to get on birth control pills without her
mother's permission.

"Psst."

Shelby and Guy were huddled behind a tall potted
palm, frantically waving her over. With a low laugh,

Faith looked conspiratorially right, then left, then joined them in their usual gathering place to exchange patient charts and any new gossip.

"Tell me one of you has something chocolate," she said hopefully.

"Is that all you think about, food?" Guy asked, and slapped his pockets. "Sorry, I've got nothing."

With a sigh, Faith pulled a granola bar from her own pocket and after splitting it three ways, stuffed her portion in her mouth. When she realized they were staring at her, she stopped in mid-chew, not easy with homemade granola. "What?"

Guy shook his head at Shelby. "She's going to deny it, so don't even bother to say anything."

"Say what?"

"Say that the sparks bouncing between you and the good Dr. Walker are threatening to burn the place down," Shelby said.

"Sparks?" Faith laughed. "Of course there's sparks. We rub each other the wrong way. I'm just sorry you're picking up on the temper between us. I know that's not good for a calm work environment."

Guy and Shelby looked at each other, then grinned.

Faith eyed them warily. "What now?"

"We're talking about *sexual* sparks, Faith," Guy told her.

"You remember the word *sexual*, right?" Shelby

lifted her brow suggestively. "Even though you haven't had any sex since the nineties."

"Don't be ridiculous." Faith forced another laugh even though, pathetically, Shelby was right. "Of course I remember...." *Sort of.* "But there's nothing between us, sexual or otherwise."

"Really? 'Cuz I could have heated my lunch burrito off the heat between you two." Guy studied his finger-nails. He'd painted the pinkies dark purple, which matched the stripe in his hair. "Probably would have burned it."

Faith's stomach growled. "You had a burrito?"

"Concentrate, hon." Shelby patted her perfect hair. "The good doctor is an amazing specimen. We know you noticed."

Faith would rather talk about burritos, extra fat please. Of course, that's why Shelby looked like a glamorous actress playing at being an overworked medical professional while Faith looked like...well, like an overworked medical professional.

"All that rough-and-tumble masculinity, combined with his take-me-as-I-am attitude. Wow." Shelby fanned herself. "And his bedside manner...made my knees weak."

"Mine, too," said Guy, also fanning himself.

"So..." Shelby, a woman who liked men as much as

Faith liked...air, looked at her. "Are you going to do him?"

Faith nearly choked on the last swallow of granola. "Not everyone is interested is 'doing' a man who is overly confident and too gorgeous for his own good."

"Speak for yourself," Guy muttered.

Shelby looked at her watch. "Look, sex is supposed to be fun. I realize you might have forgotten that, but..."

No, Faith remembered that much about sex. Barely. "I remember, but at the moment, I have to go talk to a seventeen-year-old who wants birth control pills."

Both Shelby and Guy suitably sobered. "Well, don't tell *her* how fun it is," Shelby advised. "Kids shouldn't know that."

Faith walked down the hall, practicing her abstinence speech in her head, but it seemed old-fashioned, even if she wholeheartedly believed in it for all seventeen-year-olds. But these days she had to be more realistic, and she needed to be armed with more advice than *look but don't touch*.

It turned out there wasn't just seventeen-year-old Elizabeth Stone in room seven, but her boyfriend as well, if the fact that they were thigh-to-thigh and holding hands meant anything.

Oh, and one Dr. Luke Walker, sitting right in front of them, all comfy cozy in the third patient chair. Elizabeth and the boy were smiling, and so was Luke. He was leaning back, one long leg crossed over the other, looking utterly at ease as he discussed the advantages of condoms for sex, every single time.

All three of them looked up at her when she entered, and Luke handed her Liz's chart.

"Thanks for the appointment," Elizabeth said to Dr. Walker, and with a smile at Faith, she and her boyfriend left.

Faith looked at Luke. "What are you doing?"

"Your receptionist asked me to handle some of your patients. You're backed up."

You're backed up. Not we. Of course not we, he wasn't a part of them, he was simply fulfilling what he considered a punishment by his hospital. "What did Elizabeth say?"

"She refused to discuss abstinence so we talked about STDs until she turned green. Then we talked about condoms."

Faith would've given them the same talk about sexually transmitted diseases so she had no idea why she felt the need to argue with him. Had she wanted him to disappoint her? Was she that shallow simply because *he* had been?

He yawned, and in an absent gesture, scratched his chest. Then he looked at his watch.

"Long day?"

They stood so close she could see his eyes weren't just that light see-through blue, they had specks of a darker blue dancing in them. Combined with the shadow on his jaw and his sleepy eyes, he seemed edgy, almost unbearably, effortlessly...sexy. Damn him.

And he still smelled like woodsy soap and one hundred percent perfect pure man. How annoying was that when she knew the only thing that she smelled like was disinfectant soap.

Pass the chocolate, please.

"Long *couple* of nights," he admitted, and something about the weariness in his voice caught her because she suspected this was an actual moment of vulnerability, something he didn't often show to a mere mortal like herself.

Then Shelby poked her head around the corner. "There you are. Amy Sinclair, in room three with another migraine. We've got aromatherapy and acupressure going but she asked for you, Faith."

When she was gone, she felt Luke's tension and braced herself.

"Aromatherapy." He said this like it was a bad word. "As in...candles?"

"Essential oils."

"For a migraine?"

"Or for any of a hundred other things. With essential oils you can treat sinus problems or use the oils as a sedative. Or even stimulate cell regeneration. They're also useful as an antiseptic—"

"You realize there are conventional medicines for such things."

"Conventional medicine hasn't worked for this patient."

"Have you tried—"

"Yes."

"You don't even know what I was going to say."

"She's tired of drugs, Luke." And she was tired of this argument. "She's done with the pain, and our methods are working for her. This is what she wants from us, Dr. Universe. Are you in or not?"

"*Dr. Universe?*" His eyes darkened. "What the hell does that mean?"

"It means that you, like most doctors, have a God complex."

His mouth fell open a little before he snapped it shut. Then, without another word, he turned and stalked off.

Faith waited for the surge of triumph. She'd actually won a round.

But it never came.

WHEN THE LAST PATIENT WAS gone, Faith headed toward her office. She hadn't seen Luke in a little while, not since they'd clashed again—in patient room five this time—over whether or not acupressure could ease the chronic pain of a man who'd broken his back the year before in a car accident. Luke had wanted to try muscle relaxants, but the patient, sick of drugs that didn't work, wanted to heal in a more natural way.

Luke had been gracious about it, with his usual warm bedside manner, and hadn't let one single iota of his frustration show. Not to anyone but Faith, of course, from whom he never seemed to try to hide a thing.

He was probably in the staff room now, waiting for her, brooding, pouting, and she sneaked past, heading for her office. All she wanted was five minutes on her couch with the lights off. She wanted that more than she wanted a candy bar, and that was saying something. Her head hurt, her body trembled, and she wanted to cry in frustration at the thought of getting sick now.

She opened her office door and made a beeline for her couch. She was so intent on this, it took her a moment to realize it was already taken.

Luke lay there, on his back, sprawled out, fast asleep. His feet hung off, as did one arm, making him look cramped and uncomfortable, but he lay there, head turned to the side, dead to the world.

At least he didn't snore. She eyed his long, lean,

muscular body, now dressed in those ridiculous flowered scrubs she'd given him, and had to let out a soft laugh. He made them look...fun. He'd made a lot of things look fun today, all from the viewpoint of her patients. She had to admit, the man had a way with people.

Patients, she corrected. The man had a way with patients. Not with people.

Certainly not with her.

He sighed in his sleep, and shifted, pulling his arm back up. His usually intense face was slightly softened, and...well, boyish. She could almost forget that he had a sharp tongue and even sharper wit. Almost.

His arm fell off the edge again. What a waste of incredible God-given masculinity, she thought with a roll of her eyes and nudged his foot with her own.

"What?" He sat straight up, eyes open and alert, like most medical professionals, quite used to being woken for any variety of emergencies.

"What's the matter?" he asked. The only sign of lingering grogginess was a wide yawn that revealed teeth as perfect as the rest of him.

"You're on my couch."

"Sorry." He stood, and once again stretched that long, magnificent body. "More patients?"

"No, I just need the couch." His yawn was contagious and she fought her own.

"Is that it for today then?"

"Yes. Thank you," she added. "I know we had a few differences of opinion—" He laughed, and she glared at him. "I was trying to be nice."

"What we have is more than a difference in opinion, Faith. Try *major* differences in life philosophies." His eyes met hers in a long, knowing look. "There's no prettying that up."

"But you stayed."

"Not much of a choice," he pointed out.

"Yeah, because you're a marketing nightmare."

His smile was grim. "Don't you know it."

"And because you like your position and prestige at the hospital."

He eyed her for a heartbeat during which time she wondered why in the world she was baiting the tiger. "Yes," he said eventually. "I like my position at the hospital. I like it a lot."

"So...after a day of being here, after seeing what we do for our patients, can't you maybe admit you were wrong about the clinic?"

Another long moment. "I can admit you help people," he allowed.

Was that the most she was going to get? Apparently so. And yet really, what had she expected? That he'd thank her for proving him wrong today? Yeah, right.

Exhausted, frustrated, she sank to the couch and

nearly moaned out load at the delicious body heat
he'd left her. A good amount of her resentment faded,
and snuggling in, she let out a serrated sigh.

"Good?"

"Better than good." She sighed again, softly, bliss-
fully.

His eyes heated at the sound and her tummy fluttered.

He leaned over her, a long, warm arm on either side
of her hips.

The tingle in her tummy spread. She considered
how she'd feel if he kissed her, and had just decided
she might actually let him when the blanket drifted
over her. "What are you doing?"

"Tucking you in. Need a bedtime story?"

Oh boy. "Doctor of the universe and a comedian,
too."

He tilted his head in a mocking bow.

She closed her eyes so she wouldn't stare at his
mouth, which was wide, firm, and she suspected,
quite talented. Damn distracting. Every part of him
was damn distracting. "I just want a quick catnap."

"Will it improve your disposition?"

She opened her eyes again. "Did it improve yours?"

Stunning her, he smiled, and quite frankly, it took
her breath. "My disposition is perfect," he claimed.

"Uh-huh."

His smile faded and he traced a finger over her temple, exactly where it throbbed. "Maybe..." He shifted even closer, and her heart stopped because surely this time he was going to kiss her. "Maybe you should give yourself some sort of..." He waved his hand. "Stinky treatment or something."

"Stinky?"

"You know...your smelly oils."

With a groaning laugh, she lay back. "Aromatherapy." No, she wouldn't be disappointed he hadn't leaned in and put his mouth on hers.

"Like I said, stinky stuff."

"I'm going to hold that against you."

"Yeah." He stared at her right back, an unreadable expression on his face. "I feel the same way." Then he moved toward the door, shutting it behind him.

She stared at the closed door, her heartbeat still a little unsteady. His disposition was perfect, was it? Before he'd turned on that amazing bedside manner just now she would have laughed out loud at the thought, but all she could do at the moment was feel his hands on her as he'd tucked the blanket in, the heat in his gaze as he'd run it over her, the touch of his fingers on her face... Oh, God.

She was *lusting* after Dr. Universe.

Maybe Shelby and Guy were right, maybe she just

needed sex. This thought was both thrilling and terrifying.

Emphasis on the terrifying.

LUKE DROVE HOME THAT night, going over the day in
his head. Naturopathic healing. Utilizing energy and
scents and massage for healing.

And people paid for that stuff!

It baffled him that the patients at Healing Waters
had seemed so clearly impressed with their treatments, so certain they were getting the best out there.
Not a single person had voiced discontent or bitched
at the staff. Not a single soul had left unsatisfied.

In comparison was South Village Medical Center,
where on an hourly basis someone threatened to sue,
yelled at the receptionist, or was positive the hospital
was out to get them.

He walked into his dark house, kicked off his shoes
and stripped out of his shirt. He was heading toward
the shower when his phone rang. He glanced at the
caller ID and picked up the phone to the only person
he felt like talking to at the moment, his brother.

"So, now you're a publicity nightmare," Matt said
in his ear, his voice thick with a smile. "Big surprise
there, huh? What did you say this time?"

Luke sighed. "Carmen told you."

"I called earlier. She might have mentioned it."

"Then you know what I said."

"I just wanted to hear you say it. Did you really call the hospital, the board that pays you, the idiocracy of bureaucracy?"

"Maybe." Luke rubbed the aching spot between his eyes. "Look, they let Carmen go along with a bunch of the other hospital workers, all low income, all in housekeeping. Fired them on the spot, claiming money shortages. And yet they're helping to fund this clinic with its alternative 'healing' mumbo jumbo."

"Ah. And your sense of injustice is screaming."

"*Everyone's* sense of injustice should be screaming, Matt. If they did this at *your* hospital, you'd be screaming, admit it."

"Hey, here in Texas we don't scream. We pontificate."

"I had to do something."

His brother sobered. "Yeah, I know. And it explains why Carmen is now running your life. You hired her to clean your house on a daily basis, even though you're never home to mess it up, didn't you?"

"Let's talk about you," Luke decided. "You marry your absentminded professor yet?"

"Hey, I only fell in love with Molly a week ago."

"Ah. Cold feet. Can't blame you about that one little bit. Love has never been our thing, has it?"

"I am *not* having cold feet. And love is my thing now."

"The single women in the world are weeping."

"Nah, they still have you."

Luke sighed. "It's a sad day when I have to say I'm too busy to be there for them."

"That is a sad day," Matt agreed.

"Call me after the honeymoon."

"Oh, no. When we get married, which will be soon, you'll be there."

"Weddings give me the hives."

"Too bad. You're the only family I have, Luke. The only family who ever mattered anyway."

"Yeah." Luke felt the same way, and thinking it made his voice gruff. "I'll come."

"Good. So stay out of hot water, at least until this all passes, okay?"

"It's not going to pass for three months."

"I don't suppose you can keep your mouth shut that entire time."

"Faith would love that."

"Faith? Who's Faith?"

"My boss at the clinic."

"Is she single?" Matt asked with the sudden interest of a bloodhound on the scent.

"I don't know."

"What does she look like?"

"I thought you had your woman."

"I'm thinking of you. So...is she hot?"

"Matt—"

"Hey, I just want you to be as happy as I am. So is she? Hot?"

The image of her came to mind; Faith with her long flowing red hair that never seemed to obey its restraints, her huge, expressive, and usually annoyed, green eyes, and that curvy little bod which filled out her scrubs in a way that made his hands itch. Faith...hot? Oh, yeah. "She's hot under the collar," he said carefully.

"She's hot," Matt decided with a delighted laugh.

"Goodbye, Matt."

"Are you going to ask her out?"

"Goodbye, Matt."

"You are, aren't you?"

"Good—"

"Yeah, yeah. Good luck, Luke."

With a shake of his head and a surprising smile, Luke hung up the phone. Quiet surrounded him, and his smile went nostalgic. God, he really missed having his brother around. They'd had some amazing times growing up in Texas, roaming their grandfather's fields with little to no supervision, finding trouble more often than not, but always finding it together, and suddenly, the thousand miles separating them seemed so huge. Maybe he'd take a vacation when this was over.

Right. A vacation.

He never took time off.

Well, he would, he decided. It'd be his own little reward for getting through the next two and three quarters months of Saturdays.

And one Faith McDowell.

Finishing stripping down, he showered, and was practically asleep by the time he padded naked from the bathroom straight to his bed.

Carmen had made it for him, complete with pillows neatly lined up against the headboard and the heavy comforter he never bothered with, all pulled up nice and smooth. He wasn't used to sliding into a nicely organized bed, as his mornings were usually a race to get ready while trying to remember where he'd left his keys and wallet. He couldn't spare the time to make his bed. Besides, he was just going to mess it up again at night, so he never understood the need to waste those extra few moments in the mornings.

But he had to admit, it felt good. Closing his eyes, he prepared to let sleep claim him, but for some reason, his mind once again ran over the day's events.

Despite being so busy, the clinic had run smoothly, he'd give Faith that. Her patients were carefully tended to and cared for with a personal touch he had to admit had surprised him.

Faith...

When he finally dozed off, she was *still* on his mind, and he dreamed about her healing him. Doing it with just her fingertips, healing him...when he hadn't known he needed healing.

4

FAITH HAD HER USUAL Sunday and Monday off, and since the clinic was closed, she considered a bike ride, a movie...even a shopping spree. Instead, she made the mistake of looking in her office. Seeing the stacks of paperwork waiting for her there, she ended up working both days.

On Tuesday, Healing Waters opened to slightly more patients than any time since Dr. Walker's public disdain. Wednesday, the same.

The rest of the week went by without event, other than each day showing an extremely slight increase of business, with references from the hospital and local doctors starting to pile in.

Hope among the staff surged, and Faith felt so great she didn't even crave chocolate.

By Saturday, their schedule was busting at the seams, with a shocking number of people asking to be put with Dr. Walker.

Seemed he really was a savior—theirs.

Suddenly Faith could see the light at the end of the tunnel, the day when they'd be fully operating in the black. When it got there, she'd take her first big sigh of relief since using her retirement funds to open the place. But for now, she had a lot of holding her breath left to do, and a lot of writing with red pencil on the books.

Still, the hope that had begun like a small seed in her chest earlier in the week blossomed, and she couldn't contain her smile as she came downstairs from her little apartment into the staff room.

Shelby, Guy and Catherine—their herbalist—were sitting at a table sharing wheat muffins and arguing over which one of the wildflowers in the vase in the center of the table provided the most calming effect. The muffins were clearly from Shelby—their resident health nut—and the coffee was from Guy, who needed caffeine by the bucketful.

Faith joined them, her stomach going happy, but before she stuffed in her first bite of muffin, Luke opened the back door.

Immediately the dynamics in the room changed from light and easygoing to speculative. Shelby, Guy and Cat all looked at Faith, clearly waiting for her reaction in order to decide upon theirs. So she did what she had to do even though she had no idea how she felt at the sight of him. She smiled brightly. "Well, good morning, Dr. Walker."

Looking at least far more rested than he had last Saturday, he nodded curtly. "Schedule?"

Okay, so he wasn't an easygoing, exchange-banalities kind of guy.

And he probably would rather be doing anything else today.

"Here." Shelby handed him a copy of the day's schedule, then checked her watch. "Oops, gotta run." She nudged Cat and Guy, both of whom made a big spectacle out of leaving Faith alone with Luke.

"Subtle," he said when the door shut behind them.

"Don't tell them, they think they pulled it off."

Leaning back against the counter, casually crossing one long leg over the other, looking unreasonably gorgeous and edgy in his dark trousers, and dark shirt sleeves shoved up to the elbows revealing forearms corded with strength, and big, clean hands, he studied her with an inscrutable expression. "So what's up? You going to fire me?"

Startled, she laughed. "Why would I do that?"

He lifted a broad shoulder. "Because last week we clashed over just about everything except breathing."

She looked into his light, light eyes and was startled by the vulnerability there. "We didn't clash on our passion over healing people."

"Imagine that...common ground." His gaze held hers for an immeasurable beat, during which time she couldn't have looked away to save her life. In her quest to resent him last week—resent him and need him at the same time—how had she missed the fire, the passion burning in his eyes?

"Actually," she said. "I didn't expect you to show."

"I promised three months."

"Your hospital promised."

"Same thing. I don't go back on my word."

"Even when it goes against the grain?"

"You're healing here. I'm a healer. It's what I do, it's my life." He shrugged, and with a few words, spoke volumes. "I'm here for the duration."

She'd always, *always*, been a sucker for a man in love with what he was doing with his life. She wouldn't have guessed that about Dr. Universe, and she wished she didn't know now. She didn't have time in her life for this, this…whatever it was that happened to her insides when he so much as looked at her. "We…uh, have patients."

"So it begins again."

She caught the slight quirk of his lips and wasn't as successful in hiding her own rueful smile. "It begins again," she agreed.

"Good day to you, then."

"And you." She followed him into the hallway and toward the patient rooms. And yes, maybe she stared at his very fine butt just before he shrugged into a doctor's coat, but she doubted there was a woman alive who wouldn't have done the exact same thing in her position.

"Emma Connelly," he said, studying the first chart.

"Oh, she's mine." Faith reached for the paperwork. "We have you starting with the walk-ins this morning. Room six first, there's a man waiting for you. He's suffering from allergies and—"

"It says here Emma Connelly is terminal. Ovarian cancer."

"Yes." Faith hugged the chart to her chest at the ache his words invoked. She'd known Emma for four years, watched her battle through the vicious cancer with everything she had. There was little left, and Healing Waters was dedicated to making her last days as comfortable as possible. "The aromatherapy is the only thing that eases her headaches these days. She gave up her meds, they made her so ill she couldn't function. Guy gives her therapeutic massages that keeps her muscles relaxed. The pain is so severe that—"

"There are drugs that could help. Fast acting, new drugs that—" He stopped at the look on her face and let out a disparaging breath. "Right. Shut up, Luke."

"She's tried everything. She's at the end," she said softly, her throat tight from hearing it out loud. "All she wants now is comfort. That's what we're giving her, it's all we have to give."

"Fine."

She thought that was the end of it, so when she turned away and entered the patient room, she was shocked to realize he'd followed. She introduced him to Emma, and the two of them started chatting, easily, readily.

Faith watched as Luke charmed Emma into talking about her medical history, giving him all the information he seemed to want to know, all in a genuinely relaxed conversation.

And Emma was smiling...nothing beat the sight of that. Smiling even as she shook her head over the drug methods of pain reduction that Luke tried talking to her about.

She wanted to stick with what worked for her, what soothed her, in what surely were her last days. And Faith had to give Luke credit, he never expressed disappointment or anger or any emotion at all over his advice not being taken, he simply took it in stride, then headed out to see other patients while Faith continued with Emma.

Later, Faith's shoulder brushed his as they passed each other in the hallway. "So why did you do it?" she asked, unable to let it go.

Against the wall was one of the many mini water

fountains in the clinic. Luke moved closer to it, watching the water hit the pretty rocks. "Do what?"

"With Emma. Try to bring conventional medicine into this, after I told you she wasn't interested."

He looked at her for a long moment, clearly trying to weigh his words. She wondered if he was struggling to be politically correct, so that his "punishment" wouldn't be increased.

"Knowledge is power," he finally said simply. "And I had to make sure she understood all the possible techniques, scientific or otherwise."

When she opened her mouth to remind him she'd already gone over all possible treatments with Emma, that Emma's choice had been made long before she'd even stepped foot inside the clinic, Luke put a finger over her lips.

Instantly, she went still, bombarded with sensations that had nothing to do with temper.

Heat from the rough pad of his finger.

Tingling from within her belly.

Quivering from between her thighs.

"We're going to have to agree to disagree on this," he said softly. "In fact, we're going to have to agree to disagree on just about everything." He let out a low, rough laugh. "You do know that, don't you, Faith?"

What she knew was that he'd just used her name in a silky voice, and hearing it on his lips gave the mo-

ment such a sense of intimacy, it was a drug more po-
tent than his voice, than even his smile.

Then his finger left her mouth and she was blinking
at his broad, strong shoulders as he walked away from
her, heading toward the wing where he'd do most of
his work that day, with her walk-in patients.

She let him go, a little overwhelmed by the odd and
unsettling mix of emotions he caused within her.
She'd wondered how he was going to handle the time
he had left here, but now, watching him go, with her
body in an uproar, she wondered...how was *she* going
to handle it?

SEVERAL HOURS LATER A familiar dizziness reminded
Faith she wasn't invincible. That she was still a little
run-down, an open invitation for getting sick. But
damn it, she couldn't afford to give in to this virus
right now. Stopping in the staff room, she grabbed the
turkey sandwich she'd made for lunch. And if her
stomach quietly suggested she add dessert to the
sandwich, she ignored it. She was a health professional, and she'd eat like one. Even if it killed her.

She was on her way back to her next patient when
she heard a distinct giggle. A child's giggle, which
was an irresistible sound.

It came again, and she followed it to room three.
Peeking in the ajar door, she saw a towheaded blond

boy of about five, lying on his back on the patient table, playing with an oxygen mask. He was Billy Herndon, a regular.

Next to him, also on his back, though a good part of his long, hard body hung off the other side, was one Dr. Luke Walker. He held an oxygen mask too, and they both looked at the ceiling together, playing with the equipment.

Now that Faith was closer, she could hear the rattle of Billy's breathing. Another asthma attack, a bad one given the volume of the wheezing.

"So." Luke glanced at Billy. "You think you're ready to sit with Cat now?"

"If you come."

"It's only an herbal treatment." Luke said in a perfectly natural voice, but even so, Faith nearly laughed because it was all in the man's eyes. The idea of a herbal treatment was so foreign as to be alien.

"Hey, how 'bout you go first?" Billy asked. "Then you can do it to me."

"That's Cat's job." Luke blinked innocently. "I don't want to hurt her feelings."

"But I want it to be *your* job," Billy said, adding a thrust of his lower lip. He pulled the oxygen mask away from his mouth and began wheezing again.

Gently Luke put it back in place. "How about I walk you down there, and stay with you? Deal?"

"Will you go first? You just breathe in flowers and junk. And Cat holds your hand and sings songs while you do it, funny ones about cows and bees."

Luke lifted a brow. "So you know it doesn't hurt."

The little boy smiled guiltily. "Sorta."

"Sorta." Luke ruffled his hair. "You trying to trick me, Billy?"

"Sorta."

Luke grinned. "It almost worked."

"But I still want you to do it first. Will you, Dr. Walker?" He batted his dark lashes. "Pretty please?"

"Yes, Dr. Walker," Faith said softly, coming into the room. "Pretty please?"

Lifting his head, Luke leveled his gaze on her. "Well, if it isn't Nurse McDowell. I wonder if she knows all the modern advances we've made on asthma, and how you could benefit from any of the numerous new drugs on the market?"

"Yes, but I'm lurgic to them," the boy announced proudly.

"Yes, you are," Faith said. "Very allergic. Which is why we use these other techniques."

With a sigh, Luke sat up. His hair was tousled, his eyes sleepy from lying down for so long, and right then and there, even braced for their usual disagreement, even bogged down by her annoyance at having to put up with him at all, Faith experienced another little unwanted flutter inside.

How was it possible she wanted this man?

And yet...stubborn, egotistical and single-minded as he was, he truly was amazing with her patients. As she thought it, he reached out for Billy's hand, which the boy happily gave him. "I guess," Dr. Walker said with a gusty sigh, "I could go first."

"Yippee!" Billy cried. Together they walked past Faith—both giving her a little wave, Luke adding a little brow raise to that wave, one that told her they weren't finished, not by a long shot—and out the door they went, with Billy, for the first time in recent memory, grinning.

Faith took a moment and sat, not sure if her weak knees could be attributed to not feeling great, or Luke himself. Today alone he'd brought a smile to a terminal cancer patient, a laugh to a child suffering with life-threatening asthma.

And a hitch to her own heart.

Not bad for his second week in the place.

WHEN ALL THE PATIENTS had gone for the day, Faith sat cross-legged in the center of her bed with some herbal tea and a stack of bills. Being alone was the usual state for her at night, and while occasionally she felt a little lonely, a little unsure if maybe she'd let too much of life pass her by, for the most part she was fine with her own company. After all, she was very used to it.

Her missionary parents, wonderful and loving and warm as they were, gave most of their energy away to the people they helped. Her sister, Michelle, had chosen a similar path, working as a traveling midwife in Europe.

Faith used to resent how much they gave to everyone but their own family, and yet here she sat, not doing things so very differently.

Yeah, well...if once in a while she let loneliness for family, or even a close, personal relationship encroach, she could deal with that. She'd chosen this life, and chosen it readily. Willingly. It was what she wanted.

Though what she wanted right now was to be horizontal. All she had to do was prioritize the bills for tonight and she could hit the sack. It'd been a good, solid day, and she felt happy and content with all they'd accomplished, but she could admit she was looking forward to stripping down and crawling between her fuzzy sheets. Oblivion, that's what she needed. Just six hours would do it, would beat back the viral infection she could feel at the far edges of her mind, trying as always to creep in and take hold.

She wouldn't let it. Not this time.

She had too much to do.

It was quiet downstairs. Her staff had all gone long ago. She hadn't seen Luke go, but assumed he hadn't been able to get out of there fast enough.

She'd just separated all the invoices when she heard a noise from below, a soft thud. Though she wasn't a fearful sort, she wasn't stupid. They did have supplies here, and despite Luke's mocking, they had some drugs as well. Grabbing the portable phone—with her finger on the 9-1-1 autodial—and her handy dandy baseball bat over her shoulder, she went down the stairs.

The staff room was still lit, so someone hadn't left yet. As she stood there, Luke came out of the rest room, washing his hands.

"You're still here," she said inanely.

"Just leaving." In a startlingly intimate gesture, he shifted his weight closer to hers and lifted her chin. "You have circles beneath your eyes."

"I...do?"

"You look beat to shit."

"Well, why don't you just say whatever is on your mind?" She let out an embarrassed little laugh and tried to turn away but he held her still for his inspection.

"All right. You look tired. You're not taking good enough care of yourself."

"I am so. I eat right, and I look after myself religiously."

"Yeah?" Still touching her face, his thumb slid over her skin.

Hit with a myriad of sensations from just his touch, she froze. He froze, too, all except his thumb, which went on another lazy circle. Eyes on hers, he shifted even closer.

"This," she said shakily, "is a bad idea."

"No doubt." But he gently slid his fingers into her hair and bent closer.

She leaned into him. "We should be running for the hills."

"Again, no doubt." His mouth was only a breath away. His eyes, clear and bold, never left hers.

And yet it was she who rose up on tiptoe and went to meet him halfway. Their lips met, clung for one long glorious instant before they both pulled back.

Stared at each other.

Let out two mutually shocked breaths.

At the sudden knock on the back door, Faith jumped.

"Expecting someone?" he asked.

She hadn't been expecting *him*. When she shook her head, he moved to the door and looked through the peephole. With a sudden oath, he pulled back and hauled open the door, grabbing a woman on the back step cradling her hand to her chest.

Faith recognized Luke's cleaning lady from when she'd gone to his house the week before.

"What happened?" he demanded.

The first litany that exploded from Carmen came in Spanish.

"English, English," Luke urged, reaching out to support her hand, which came away from her chest bloody.

"*English?*" she sputtered. "How's this for English? Your damn fancy window in the living room was stuck open, and it looked like rain so I had to climb—" She sucked in a harsh breath. "Don't squeeze it, you idiot!"

With one arm around her, the other supporting her hurt hand, he moved past Faith and went inside. "Let me look at you."

"You must have painted that stupid window open," Carmen said. "Big surprise there, eh? Big hotshot doctor who can't hammer a nail? The wind started bringing in dirt—"

"Carmen—"

"And damn you, I'd spend the afternoon dusting—"

"Shut up. Carmen, this is Faith McDowell. Faith, Carmen."

"Nice to see you again. I'm not doing windows anymore, you thankless bastard," Carmen said, and beyond the temper in her voice, Faith heard genuine pain.

"If I'm so thankless why did you come looking for me instead of going to the E.R.?"

"Because they're crooks."

Still holding on to Carmen, he looked at Faith. "She needs stitches."

"Stitches? Well, *that* explains why there's spots spinning in front of my eyes..." Carmen clamped her mouth shut as the whites of her eyes flashed.

"Perfect," Luke grunted as she fainted, scooping up her lifeless body in his arms. "Lead the way before I collapse from the dead weight."

Humor. Faith hadn't imagined he had any. Racing ahead of him, flipping on lights as they went, she led the way to a patient room.

And over the next hour, as he stitched Carmen's hand, he showed Faith a lot of that humor as he dealt with Carmen's medical phobia in the most heartbreaking, tender way she could have imagined.

"Elevate it," she said to Carmen at the exact same time Luke did.

He looked at her. "I'm going to prescribe painkillers, too. Want to say it in tandem?"

"I'm not against painkillers," she said so primly he laughed.

"Wow. Stop the world. We agree again." Hands on his hips, he turned to Carmen and let out a long-suffering sigh. "I suppose you'll need a ride."

Carmen swore at him in Spanish, then sniffed. "*Si*, I took a cab here."

When Luke got her to the back door, he stopped and looked at Faith. "Thanks for letting me treat her here after hours. Just bill me. I've got to get her to my car now." He was supporting all her weight. "She's going to break my back."

Carmen used her good hand to hit him upside the head.

Luke grinned. "See? You're feeling better already."

Faith held the door open. "So...see you next Saturday."

His gaze met hers over the top of Carmen's head. The humor was gone now, and suddenly she braced herself. He was going to say he wasn't coming back.

Which, really, would be fine. More than fine. They rubbed each other the wrong way, they...also rubbed each other the right way.

"Next week," he agreed softly, and then he was gone, leaving her staring out into the night, wondering if she felt relieved...or terrified.

ON MONDAY MORNING LUKE was called into Leo's office at the hospital. "Good news," his friend boomed.

"Faith McDowell gave you a glowing recommendation. You must have made quite an impression these last two weeks, with all those hot oil therapies and healing touches."

Luke opened his mouth, saw the twinkle in Leo's eyes and relaxed. "Sure. Make fun. You're not the one having to give up two and a half months more of Saturdays."

"You don't either."

"What?"

Leo lifted a brow. "She released you. Said that while she was impressed with your grasp of alternative healing techniques—"

Luke snorted.

Leo shot him a long look. "You don't need to fulfill the rest of your time at the clinic."

Faith had released him from his duty.

This was just about the last thing he expected. He waited for the elation. For the satisfaction. For the sheer overwhelming relief.

Leo laughed at his confusion. "I thought you'd be dancing in the hallways at the news."

"Yeah." Luke walked the length of the office and looked out the window. Dancing in the hallways? He would, but suddenly his stomach had fallen to a region somewhere near his toes. "Leo—"

Leo's pager went off. "Sorry, gotta run."

Yeah. So did Luke. The E.R. was full and they were short staffed. Over the rest of the day he removed two spleens, set a broken hip, stitched up a motorcyclist...and never stopped thinking about Healing Waters. Faith.

Why had she released him? She needed him, she'd said so. She needed his visible, public support. She needed the free additional medical staff. She needed...him.

He couldn't shake it, which was the only reason he stopped by the clinic after his shift instead of going home. It had nothing, nothing at all, to do with wanting to see her again.

No one answered his knock downstairs, but that made sense as the clinic was always closed on Mondays. Going around the back, he took the stairs, which were lined with potted plants. On her porch sat a comfy looking wooden swing. Her back door had a large window in it, lined with lace, which allowed him a clear look into her lit kitchen.

And what his clear look afforded him stopped his heart.

Faith, slumped on the floor.

5

LUKE FUMBLED FOR Faith's door. Finding it locked, he stepped back, then charged it. With far less brute strength than he could have imagined, the door shuddered open.

She hadn't budged. She had her back to the cabinets, her arms around her drawn-up knees and her head down, and was far too still.

He dropped to his knees beside her. "Faith."

Slowly, as if it hurt to move, she lifted her head. Her face was ashen, and when he cupped her jaw in his shaking hands, she was damp with sweat. "Don't touch me," she said. "I'm getting sick."

He slid his hand through a tangle of long red hair. "The flu?" He stroked her hair from her face, felt her forehead. She was cool, even cold.

"It always happens when I let myself get run down. It's an old virus, and I felt it coming for two weeks. I'm all shaky and dizzy. Damn it."

He might have smiled at her petulant tone, if his heart wasn't still threatening to burst right out of his chest. "You don't have a fever."

"So?"

"So when did you eat last?"

Scowling at him, she pushed him away and made to get up, but he slid his hands to her hips and held her down.

She glared at him.

"Stay." Surging to his feet, he went to her refrigerator and pulled out a carton of orange juice. He brought it to her. "Drink."

"From the carton?" she asked with such horror he laughed.

"Just a few sips."

"I'd rather have some tea. You don't by any chance know how to make purple coneflower tea?"

"Huh?"

"Echinacea. It's used to boost the immune system, and also as an antibiotic."

Luke just stared at her.

"Oh, never mind." Leaning her head back against the counter, she tipped the carton up and took a swig.

He watched a drop escape her lips and glide down her chin, gaining momentum and hitting a breast. For some oddly inappropriate reason, his mouth watered. He swallowed hard. "Still dizzy?"

"Yeah."

"Then keep your eyes open." He kept his gaze on hers. With his hands already on her body, it was the safest route, though it was a little shocking to realize he needed a safe route. "It'll help."

When she shot him a daggered look, he lifted a shoulder. "Hey, once a doctor..." He watched her take another sip of juice, and some color came back into her cheeks. Satisfied, he leaned back on his heels and let out a breath. "Well. That was fun."

"Sorry." Leaning back against the counter, she studied the ceiling. "You can give me some room now."

Yeah. Yeah, he probably could. Clearly she didn't want him hovering any more than he wanted to hover, so he scooted back a bit.

Better. Definitely better.

Too bad he couldn't forget the feel of her in his hands, and doubted he would anytime soon.

"Did you break my door?"

"Easily. Christ, Faith, anyone could break in here."

"Well, lucky for me, no one but you wanted to." Staggering to her feet, she shoved her hair out of her face and sighed. "I feel a little better."

He opened his mouth to say something to that, something pithy he was certain, but she narrowed her eyes on him. "So why are you here?"

"I—" He blinked. Why had he come? He looked into her green, green eyes and tried to remember. "You told the hospital you don't need me anymore."

She stared at him, then let out a low laugh. "And that bothered you? I thought you'd be celebrating."

"Why, Faith?"

"Why? My God, Luke." She scrubbed her hands over her face and finally dropped them to her sides, looking tired, so very tired he had to fight the urge to move close again. To put his hands back on her and—

"Look, I'm not up for this." Still looking a bit too shaky for his comfort, she moved to the open door, and waited expectantly for him to obey her silent command and scram.

"Gee," he said. "I guess we're done talking."

"So done."

"Are you always cranky when you don't eat?"

"I told you, I have a vir—"

"Virus," he said at the same time as her, and shaking his head, he moved to the door and shut it. "So." He leaned into her, and yet again his pulse jumped, and so did hers. He could see it beating furiously at the base of her throat. "Is it really that you don't feel good, or was it the shock of attraction when I touched you?"

Her mouth tightened, but she remained stubbornly mute.

"Yeah," he said softly. "Thought so."

"You are the most egotistical man I've ever met."

"Egotistical?" He let out a rough laugh. "Faith, I put

my hands on you in a purely nonsexual way and it jolted me to my toes. Is it 'egotistical' to admit that terrifies me?''

She bit her lower lip, a sexy little gesture that didn't help matters any. "Okay, maybe I felt it, too. A little."

"A little," he repeated. For a reason completely unknown to himself, he stroked her jaw. "What are we going to do about it?"

"Nothing, nothing at all. I'm too busy, and you... you're back to your own life, Dr. Universe. Thanks for the help the last two weekends, but your services are no longer needed or required."

Since he spent most of his life being needed in one form or another, this should have been a welcome break. She was right, he should be celebrating. "Fine."

"Fine."

Now he felt tense again. "You really feeling better?"

"Sure."

Yeah, and he was Santa Claus. "What did you last eat?"

"I had a nice big pasta salad for lunch, a good healthy snack of carrots—"

"Dinner, Faith. Something with protein."

"By dinner I was sick," she admitted. "I didn't want to eat."

"You need a keeper, you know that?"

"I've been on my own for a long time. For forever. I'm my own keeper."

"Well then, damn it, do a better job. Where's your family?"

"Africa, if you must know. They're missionaries. And before you ask, I have a sister, but she's in Europe. She works as a traveling midwife there."

So she was as alone as he was. "They're as dedicated as you."

"More. They give everything they have to their jobs, over everything else. At least I still manage to have a life."

"Really? When?"

She looked away. "Sometimes."

He didn't like the hint of sadness in her eyes, or the knowledge that her parents had put their work ahead of their children, much the way his own had. "And so you're completely alone." The way he was. Damn it, why had he started this conversation?

"I have the clinic."

Yeah, the clinic. Which brought them full circle. "Just tell me why you released me from my duties here."

"You're a smart man," she whispered, stepping back, away from his touch. "You figure it out."

"But—"

"Good night, Luke." With a gentle shove, she put him back out into the night.

The door shut behind him, but when he turned, there was a definite gap between the wood and the jamb. He stared at it uneasily. "Put a chair beneath the knob," he said to the wood. "And I'll send someone to fix that lock tomorrow."

"Good night, Luke."

"A chair," he repeated, and stood there until he heard her do it, then with a long, pent-up breath, drove home.

You're a smart man, you figure it out.

But he didn't, not until hours and hours had passed, during which time he'd tossed and turned in his bed, watching the shadow of the moon play across the ceiling.

Finally, with the rising sun, he got it. She'd released him from his duties for the exact same reason he'd been so afraid to go back.

It was that undeniable something between them, a spark neither of them could ignore, and neither wanted. More importantly, there was a need.

He needed her.

He, Luke Walker, who did his damn best not to need anyone else, *needed* her.

A FEW SLEEPLESS NIGHTS later, Luke sat in front of his television with no idea what was on. His head hurt, his mind was full of things; work mostly, and the incredible miracles they'd performed at the hospital all week, and also his brother's upcoming wedding, which was now definitely set for summer.

He was Matt's best man, which was okay, even if a part of him was still baffled over how his brother could possibly want to sleep with the same woman for the rest of his life.

Damn, he needed ibuprofen. Too bad he was out of them. A doctor who couldn't heal his own headache. Sad.

Tomorrow was Saturday. A day he should have dedicated to one redheaded, temperamental, beautifully infuriating Faith McDowell because of his own big mouth.

But she'd politely set him free.

Which really, as Leo had said, should have sent him dancing down the hallways. And it would, if his head didn't still feel as if it was going to fall right off his shoulders.

When he heard the knock at his door, he turned off the TV. Maybe if he was really quiet, whoever it was would go away. Far away.

Another knock didn't improve the pounding in his head, so he got up. The last person in the world he expected, and the one person on his mind, stood there wearing a flowery sundress and strappy sandals.

Faith McDowell, so tough and in charge of her world, had pink toenails and a dainty little silver toe ring.

"Hi." She let out a little smile. "Am I interrupting anything?"

"Nothing but a king-size headache."

"Really?" She cocked her head and sent him a sympathetic look. "I could fix that for you."

"You have ibuprofen? I'm completely out, and too lazy to go to the store."

"I don't need pills."

"Hmm." He eyed her. "You have fairy dust?"

"Maybe." She reached for his hand. "Let me get rid of the headache for you, Luke."

He felt the pull of her touch like a thousand watts as she led him into his own house. Did she feel it, he wondered as he followed her like an eager puppy, watching her slim, straight spine, her hips swaying in a way that made his aching head spin.

She craned her neck when he slowed his steps, and her hair wildly flowed around her bare shoulders. "Problem?"

Hell, yes. "No. No problem."

She sent him a smile from beneath lowered lashes

that revealed nothing of her true thoughts. "Then what's the slowdown? You chicken?" she taunted.

Her voice was low, sexy, and he doubted that was intentional. Still, the teasing lightened his own troubled thoughts. "Hell, yeah, I'm chicken. There's a reason *I* always wear the doctor's coat."

"It'll only take a minute for me to make you feel better, I promise." She pushed him down to his coach and stood over him, her hands on her hips.

His eyes hungrily traveled up the length of her curvy, lush body. "Is it gonna hurt?" he asked, only half kidding.

"Not if you believe."

He nearly swallowed his tongue when she dropped to her knees on the floor beside him, head now level with the part of his body coming to hopeful attention. Complicating matters, she put her hand on his thigh.

From her shockingly innocent yet unbearably erotic position, with her hair brushing his knee, she smiled. "Put your hand on your thigh," she instructed. "Palm up."

"Uh..." He was getting more intelligent by the moment.

"Just try it," she said in that voice that brought to mind hot, wild sex on silk sheets by moonlight.

Just try it. He set his hand as directed on his thigh.

"Close your eyes."

"Faith—"

"Close 'em, doc."

At least she'd left off the Universe endearment. Slowly, feeling...strangely aware, he closed his eyes.

After a heartbeat, her finger ran over his, lightly, and he relaxed.

"Good," she whispered. "Let go. Let it all go."

Her voice was hypnotic, and he loosened up even more. Then, suddenly, he felt a pinch in the fleshy part of his hand between his thumb and pointer finger, and his eyes flew open. "Ouch!"

Faith shook her head and laughed. "Oh, please. I barely squeezed." She held the pressure steadily, her eyes holding his. "Let out your breath," she demanded softly, "Don't stop breathing... What do you feel?"

He felt her hands on his. He felt her soft breath on his arm, he felt her breast pressing into his leg, and suddenly he couldn't remember what she'd asked, though she was clearly waiting on an answer. "Um...what?"

She lifted a brow. "Is the pain eased?"

The dull throbbing in his head was indeed eased and he blinked in confusion.

She laughed. Just tossed her head back and laughed, the sound full and throaty, and so damned sexy he nearly tumbled himself down on the floor to be right next to her.

"Oh, Luke. If you could see your face." She was still grinning. "Such shock. What's the matter, you've never eased an ache without a little pill?"

"All you did was use a pressure point."

"Well, give the man an A plus. And welcome to acupressure, an alternative and effective way of healing." She shifted, preparing to stand, but for just a flash, a very dizzy flash, she stayed on her knees practically between his, a hand braced on his thigh, and all the blood in his head drained. A sound escaped him, one that sounded rough and...needy.

Suddenly wide-eyed, she stared at him. Licked her lips in a nervous, artless gesture that made him groan.

Startled at the second sound ripped from his throat, she went to move away, but he grabbed her wrist, halting her exit.

Her hand came up between them for balance, pressing against his chest, and for a long moment they just looked at each other. Slowly, he took her hands and linked their fingers, then moved their joined hands to the small of her back. Nudging her forward, into the V of his spread legs, into his hips, he let out another groan.

She relaxed her stiff body against his, and sighed. With pleasure? God, he wished he knew, because he was dying of it. With a purely physical response, he rocked against her.

A little sound escaped her now, one that managed to perfectly convey her bewildered arousal. Her fingers curled into his.

Then suddenly she stood, and he was staring at her nicely rounded ass as she moved away, toward the door.

"Faith? Where are you going?"

"Home."

"But..." Rising, he moved after her, and caught her at the door. "You never said why you came."

She nibbled on her lower lip, that nervous little gesture he found fascinating. "I wanted to thank you for the other night. You were being so kind and I..."

"Was being grumpy?"

That coaxed out a smile. "Yeah."

"You feel better?"

"I do."

They stood staring at each other for a long, awkward beat. Slowly Luke shook his head. "What?" Faith whispered.

He laughed. "Half the time you drive me out of my living mind, you know that? I mean we think so differently, we work differently, we do everything differently."

"And...the other half of the time?"

Shaking his head, he lifted a hand and traced her jaw. "The other half of the time you still drive me out of my living mind, but...not necessarily with irritation."

"Yeah, well, it's that other half we need to be careful of." She stepped back so that his hand fell away from her soft skin. "And that's the half we need to get over."

"Right."

She reached behind her for the door handle. With no little amount of wariness, she met his gaze. "I know why I need to get over it, but I was wondering...about you. Is it because I'm not an M.D.?"

"No! Of course not."

"Is it because I moved past conventional medicine?"

"No." He looked into her beautiful eyes, into the still wary expression and wondered why this was so hard. Being honest had never been hard before. Hurting people's feelings had never been hard before. But the truth, that he had his life just the way he wanted it, that if he dallied with a woman these days, it was just that, a dalliance, and she wasn't the type of woman to be happy with that, seemed...lame. "It's complicated."

"Yeah." Her face fell and she turned to walk out the door.

"Faith—"

"It's best if I go."

He watched her hightail it out of his place, and struggled to remember how right she was. They needed to get over whatever this...this thing was, because it had no place in his life. She had no place in his life.

If only he could remember why that was exactly.

SATURDAY MORNING DAWNED bright and early. Faith felt rested and ready to work. She told herself she'd had such a good-night's sleep because this was a Dr. Universe-free weekend. He was out of her life. She had no worries, no worries at all.

But then Guy called in sick. So did her receptionist. And Cat, too.

All three struck down with the flu, possibly the same thing she'd had earlier in the week. Faith talked to them each on the telephone, assuring them she'd be fine, that they needed to worry only about getting better. She reminded them to drink their echinacea tea and get lots of rest.

Then she got off the phone and looked at Shelby. "We're screwed."

"Maybe I should start calling the scheduled patients, cancel them."

That would go over great, just when they were starting to garner a steady clientele, just when—

The back door opened and, as if he'd been sent from heaven, in walked Luke.

"Morning," he said to their startled faces.

When they continued to just stare at him, he lifted his covered coffee mug, still steaming, and looked at it. "I know it's not any fancy tea, and that it's store-bought, but a guy's gotta have his vices."

"Are you...here to *work?*" Shelby asked. "Because if you are, I'll kiss you, right here, right now."

"I'm here to work, yeah, if you don't mind. No kiss required."

"Mind?" Shelby laughed. "Do we mind, Faith?"

Did she? Ha! Luke was watching her, waiting, and the silence stretched out.

"Okay, she's not going to admit this because she's stubborn as hell," Shelby confided. "But I'll tell you. We're short-staffed and overbooked today."

Luke never took his eyes off Faith. "Really."

"Yeah, and another thing she won't tell you, if you hadn't shown up, we'd have had to turn away patients."

"Ouch."

"Ouch," Shelby agreed, then caught Faith's glaring expression. "Oops, would you look at the time? Better get moving."

Faith watched Shelby leave, then turned on Luke. "Okay, why are you really here?"

"Last I checked I was a doctor, willing and able to work."

"Yes, but you're not required to work here anymore, remember?"

"I remember." He slid his hands into his pockets, rocking back on his heels. "I also remember I like to repay my debts."

"There's no debt."

"Yes, there is." He let out a slow breath and his shoulders dropped slightly. "Look, even though the newspapers exaggerated what I said, I spoke without the facts when I talked about this place. And if you think that's easy to admit, think again. I still believe in scientific and conventional medicine, I still believe that what I do, what the hospital does, can't be replaced by alternative methods of medicine. But I *can* admit..."

"Yes?"

"That what you're doing here has a place. That it's important to the people you see." He turned in a slow, frustrated circle, one hundred and eighty pounds of tightly coiled male. "And I did you a great disservice by so carelessly shrugging it off. People listen to us, they listen to me. So in light of that, I want to keep

working here, for the rest of the two months, or whatever it is."

"Two months, one week."

"Two months, one week," he repeated slowly. "For
that long, people can see I believe in what you're doing."

"Even if *you* don't believe?"

He winced. "Why can't you just be happy to see
me?"

"Maybe I am," she whispered, and had the satisfaction of rendering him speechless.

IT WASN'T LIKE BEFORE, working with Luke. Before,
they'd not talked, not really. They certainly hadn't
touched.

Or kissed.

But now, every time they passed in the hallway,
brushed shoulders or hands, no matter how accidentally, it brought it all back.

The tension grew between them, tighter and tighter,
until it became this tangible thing she could have
reached out and touched.

Throughout the day, it only got worse. Going in to
see a woman with severe arthritis, they'd accidentally
bumped shoulders in the doorway. It had taken her
breath. *He'd* taken her breath, so much she nearly forgot how to treat the woman's arthritis.

They saw a nine-months pregnant woman suffering false labor pangs thanks to the can of olives she'd consumed, and leaving the room together, they'd brushed hands....

Faith's legs had tightened. So had her nipples.

Had he noticed?

Hard to tell, but she would have sworn on her life that his breathing changed every time he caught her staring at him.

Probably nothing more than regret that he'd come back. Yeah, that had to be it, because surely he didn't feel as she did, as if she were a firecracker with a lit fuse. She could hardly look into his eyes, afraid he'd see it. She certainly couldn't talk to him. In fact, she'd avoided being anywhere near him for over an hour now, thinking that would help.

It hadn't.

A little off balance, she entered the storage closet, planning on restocking, catching her breath—

But suddenly, Luke was in there with her, crowding into her space, looking at her in a way that made all the thoughts scatter right out of her head.

He took the stack of fresh towels out of her unresisting hands, then with mouth grim and tense, slid his hands to her shoulders and backed her to a wall.

"Wh—what are you doing?"

"What I should have done long before now," he growled, and crushed his mouth down on hers.

6

THE INTENSE, SIZZLING HEAT had been building between them all day. So much so, that having Luke's
mouth on hers now, after thinking about it, dreaming
about it, made her come just a little undone, just
enough that she didn't care that they stood in an open
closet, hands grappling for purchase on each other's
bodies, the passion growing between them by leaps
and bounds.

Then Luke pulled back and stared at her. "What the
hell is this?"

"I have no idea..."

Swearing reverently, he came at her again, as if he
meant to inhale her.

She let him. Wanted him. "More."

"Yeah." Luke slid his hands down her sides,
gripped her hips, pushed her back to a shelving unit,
pressing his body along the length of hers. "More."

Again, when they needed air, they pulled back,
gasping, staring, then unable to keep apart, lunged at
each other yet again. A stack of paper gowns rained
over them, then some other supplies, but nothing mat-

tered save this. It was delicious, brain-cell destroying, and she needed more, still more. Shoving him around so she could press *him* against the shelving unit as he had done to her, she raced her hands up his chest, around his neck...fisted them in his hair.

More supplies fell. She didn't care. She'd have crawled up his body if she could, and given the low, rough growl that came from deep in his throat, he felt the same way.

Arching into him, she lifted a leg, tried to wrap it around his hip. He whipped them around again, pressed her hard to the wall. "Yeah. God." Gripping her thigh, he held her open to his slow, purposeful thrust.

Her head thunked back, hit the wall.

He ate at her neck; hot, wet, openmouthed bites that had her whimpering, gasping for more but neither of them spoke, words weren't necessary. Nothing was necessary except this, not even air.

Obeying the vicious need, she simply melted into him as he continued to ravage, a long, deep, wet, devouring kiss that cloaked them in intimacy, in desperate, hungry desire. She kissed him back the same way, giving everything she had, her mouth open to meet his in a mindless beat out of time, slipping her hands beneath his shirt and over his smooth, sleek back, rippled with tension.

His fingers opened the white lab coat she wore and danced beneath her blouse, over the quivering muscles of her belly, then higher, to just the bottom curves of her breasts.

Her toes curled. Her nipples had long ago hardened into two aching buds. And what was happening between her thighs required the same attention as a five-alarm fire. Arching up into him as much as she could, irresistibly drawn by the slow, sexy forays of his tongue into her mouth, she moaned.

Slow and deliberate, he continued to kiss her, spreading the aching heat in her belly, in her breasts, between her thighs.

But then he drew back, just a fraction of an inch, and chest heaving, stared at her as if he'd never seen her before.

She felt the same way. "I...I'm not sure where that came from."

"Yeah." He was breathing too hard, so was she, she could hear the air chopping in and out of both their lungs. His hands slid down to curl into her hips, holding her against his rock-hard body.

Her hands were still tangled in his dark, silky hair.

Not an inch separated chest or belly or thighs, as she stood there weaving slightly, flushed with passion and quivering with need.

He looked as shell-shocked as she felt. "I should tell

you," he said. "I've been thinking about that for a while now." His voice was rough and scratchy. And so damned sexy she could close her eyes and listen to him for the rest of the day.

Instead, she stared into his light blue eyes and saw more questions than answers. "I thought we figured this for a bad idea."

"Oh, it is. A really, really bad idea." Too bad Luke wasn't thinking with his heart at the moment.

Or even his brain.

It made no sense, no sense at all, why just looking at her made him ache all the time, why the feel of her beneath his hands nearly drove him wild.

Maybe it'd been too long since he'd had sex, but that was just an excuse. It was her, Faith, and horrifying or not, he'd have to face that.

Later. Much, much later.

"Luke..." She licked her lips and made him groan. Stared at his mouth and made his knees weak.

"I know." But he didn't, not really. He didn't have a clue, and he badly needed one.

"Are we going to do that again?"

"No." But he captured her mouth again anyway, because not getting another taste of her, when the first was still driving him out of his living mind, wasn't an option.

Her lips parted with a soft moan, and then her

hands moved on his bare, heated flesh. Having her hands on him, hearing her pant softly, helplessly, drove him straight to the edge. He opened his mouth wider, pressing himself into her, letting out a low, rough groan when her fingers dug into his skin as if she needed the grip on her faltering reality. She was so unexpectedly irresistible, so damned fascinating, he couldn't let her go.

It was shocking, how much he needed this, shocking and delicious, and carried the pack of a one-two punch. He hadn't come for this, damn it, he'd come just to do his time. He didn't fully understand this clinic, or the sense of hope it gave to patients he still felt could be better served by conventional medicine, and yet here he was, his mouth and hands fully occupied—

"The door," she said into his mouth. "Luke, the door—"

Unbelievably, it was still open. More unbelievably, no one had caught them. Without breaking their connection, he kicked it closed and backed Faith to it, cradling her face and kissing her until the world receded again, until there was nothing, no one, except this, her.

She pulled her hands out from his shirt. He nearly moaned at the loss but, then she unbuttoned it, spread it open.

He shoved the lab coat off her shoulders, then her blouse.

She bit his bare shoulder.

He cupped her breasts in his hands.

And the world tilted.

"Lust," she gasped, when they next came up for air.

He might as well have just run a marathon for all his ability to breathe. He had a mouthful of her throat, a handful of her perfect breasts and his leg thrust high between hers. "Huh?"

"Lust." She licked her lips, that gesture he found so sexy, and like a helpless slave to the hunger, he thrust his hips against hers.

"It's...just lust," she repeated.

"Are you sure?" Because, shockingly enough, suddenly he wasn't.

"Extremely." She didn't look it though. "We've already decided we're just too different, right? Too busy with our own lives."

He slowly blinked. That's right. Too busy.

"I mean, obviously we have a thing for each other. A chemical thing. I can't seem to take my hands off you, and vice versa—"

At the reminder of where his hands were, cupped over her breasts, his thumbs rasping her nipples, he nearly groaned again. Instead, he slid them down, squeezing her hips now, and when she thrust against him one more time, he dropped his hands even further, to cup her perfectly rounded bottom.

Her eyes were opaque with desire, her voice a little shaky. "I'm thinking we can handle this." She wet her lips. "Lust is just a bodily function, right? Like drinking or going to the bathroom. So...we just deal with it. Then go on our merry way."

"Deal with it." Thinking on his feet had never been more difficult. "So you're saying we should..."

"Well, not here."

He looked around. Right. They were in a storage closet. At the clinic. With patients just down the hall.

Good God.

"But after work..."

He stared down into her still-flushed face. Her hair had rioted. Her blouse was opened and her nipples pressed enticingly against the material of her bra, seriously hampering his ability to put words together. "Are you trying to say we *should* have sex?"

"Just on Saturdays. For the two months you're so honor bound to give me."

He blinked again. "I thought we were going to ignore this."

"Are we ignoring it now?"

No. No they weren't. Of their own accord, his fingers again tightened on her very delectable ass. Ignore her? He had maybe a snowball's chance in hell. "What about after the two months?"

She bit her full lower lip again. "Well...you'd just have to let me go. I'm sorry, Luke, but like we said, we're just too different."

Too different? Right. They were too different.

Any red-blooded man would be laughing in triumph at this unexpected offer, any single man he knew. Hell, any man in the entire free universe.

Did he have this correct? Could he possibly? This gorgeous, sexy, unbelievably hot woman wanted to have sex with him, then after two months of great—and it would be great—sex, just walk away, all without a diamond ring, a white dress, white cake or white picket fence.

Oh yeah, he should be doing the happy dance. But he didn't feel like dancing. "Faith...you deserve more than that."

"It's what I want." She arched, very slightly, letting her extremely tight, hot nipples rub against his chest. "Are you going to turn me down, Luke? Are we going to have to try to work together, all worked up, without any relief?"

The thought made him want to cry. "No. God, no."

She smiled, backed away. "We probably have patients."

"Patients."

"I'll go first. I'll—"

A pounding at the door had them both jumping.

"Faith? Is that you in there?" Shelby called. "We have a patient we want to consult on, room four. You in there?"

"Uh..." Faith's eyes widened on Luke. "Yes. Yes, I'm in here."

"Well, open up." The knob turned, but before it could open, Luke wedged his foot against it.

"Faith? Are you *stuck* in there?"

Faith let out a slow, careful breath, and so did Luke. "Uh...not exactly."

"What are you doing?"

"Well..." Faith grinned at Luke, and right then and there, with his foot blocking the door so that they wouldn't get caught, with his shirt ripped open and hers half off her body as well, he fell a little bit in love.

"Faith?"

"I'll...be out in a minute!"

"Okay..." Shelby's voice went to a low, conspirator's whisper. "Do you have Dr. Walker in there with you?"

Wide-eyed, she stared at Luke. "Uh..."

"Oh my God. You do...okay, you know what? Never mind, I'll figure out the patient situation in room four. You two just...carry on."

Her footsteps moved away and Luke realized Faith

was still staring at him, a little hopefully now, and he let out a rough groaning laugh. "No," he whispered. "We're not carrying on, not in this closet."

With a sigh, she started straightening her clothes.

He looked down at himself and tried to figure out if a doctor's coat could possibly cover the biggest erection he'd ever had.

"So, have we come to terms?"

He stopped in the act of tucking in his shirt and looked at her. "Terms?"

"About...you know."

"Sleeping together?"

She shook her head. "Actually, sleeping would be a bad idea."

His head was spinning. "But you just said..."

"*Sleeping* implies some sort of relationship, when we both know a relationship between us would never work. In fact," she said earnestly, "sleeping together would only backfire."

"Right. Backfire." And she was right. Hell, she was so right. He'd gotten sidetracked in her glorious body, but the truth was staring him in the face. He didn't want a relationship, and neither did she. So why his hands itched to grab her close again and talk her into exactly that was beyond him.

She finished buttoning herself up—though not correctly—and scooped her hair up off her face, holding it there with some clip she pulled out of her pocket. Immediately, strands of long red hair escaped, making her look like...like she'd just been in the storage closet being ravaged. "I'll see you," she whispered and turned from him to reach for the door.

Let her go.

Instead, he grabbed her and turned her back to him. Reaching out, he fixed the buttons on her blouse. The woman needed a goddamn keeper. Not a job he wanted to apply for. Nope. He was going to walk away. Hell, he was going to run—

She kissed his cheek, sent him a smile that made his heart tumble in his side. "Thanks."

Then she was gone.

Luke stood in that closet for a good long time, until his coat was no longer tented with his obvious hard-on. Until he'd decided that yes, the right thing was to walk out of the closet and right out the front door of the clinic.

So he walked out of the closet.

Walked down the hall.

And then turned right instead of left, and went to see which patients needed his attention.

THAT NIGHT, FAITH SAT alone on her couch staring at the wall. She'd done yoga, had given herself an aromatherapy session and had eaten dinner with Shelby.

Play the Lucky Hearts Game

and get...

2 FREE BOOKS
and a **FREE MYSTERY GIFT...**
YOURS to KEEP!

yes! I have scratched off the silver card. Please send me my **2 FREE BOOKS** and **FREE mystery GIFT**. I understand that I am under no obligation to purchase any books as explained on the back of this card.

Scratch Here!
then look below to see what your cards get you... 2 Free Books & a Free Mystery Gift!

▼ **DETACH AND MAIL CARD TODAY!** ▼

342 HDL DU62   142 HDL DU7J

FIRST NAME

LAST NAME

ADDRESS

APT.#

CITY

STATE/PROV.

ZIP/POSTAL CODE

(H-T-08/03)

Twenty-one gets you
2 FREE BOOKS
and a **FREE MYSTERY GIFT!**

Twenty gets you
2 FREE BOOKS!

Nineteen gets you
1 FREE BOOK!

TRY AGAIN!

BUSINESS REPLY MAIL
FIRST-CLASS MAIL   PERMIT NO. 717-003   BUFFALO, NY

POSTAGE WILL BE PAID BY ADDRESSEE

HARLEQUIN READER SERVICE
3010 WALDEN AVE
PO BOX 1867
BUFFALO NY 14240-9952

NO POSTAGE
NECESSARY
IF MAILED
IN THE
UNITED STATES

None of the normally calming, soothing rituals had soothed her. Nope, she was keyed up, strung tighter than a cheap guitar, and for once it wasn't nerves or anxiety over money or the clinic.

She'd thrown herself at Luke today.

She'd like to blame the heat of the moment, especially with his mouth on hers and his hands...oh goodness, his hands. Things had gotten so fiery so fast in that storage closet, they'd practically singed off any unwanted body hair with the fire they'd generated.

Yeah, blaming the heat of the moment sounded like a good excuse for how shameless she'd been. How else could she explain offering him sex for the next two months?

So damn it, where was he? She looked out the window. The only car in the lot below was hers.

He should be here now, easing her tension with his hands, his mouth, his body.

Why wasn't he?

But after the last patient had gone, so had he.

And here she sat, alone, thinking about sex until her body hummed.

Only a few weeks ago she'd have said that sex, no matter how consensual, how healthy, should never be used outside a loving, monogamous relationship. But only a few weeks ago she hadn't met Luke Walker.

With a sigh, she got ready for bed alone, and plopped onto her mattress.

And then proceeded to stare at the ceiling imagining all she could be doing if Luke had shown up.

Since sleep wasn't going to come—and neither was she or Luke apparently—she padded downstairs in her oversize T-shirt and favorite bunny slippers to hit the paperwork until she felt suitably tired.

Flipping on the light in her office had her blinking like an owl. Her desk was definitely threatening to bust at the seams. Looking at the stack of unpaid bills, her tummy flip-flopped. It would be nice to have someone to call right now, right this minute, someone to talk to, someone who understood her, through thick and thin.

But her mother and father, while wonderful, giving people, had never really been the kind she could go running to. They dealt with people who needed them on a daily basis, and in return, expected more of their offspring.

She supposed she could call her sister, but the truth was, Faith didn't even have a contact phone number for her. That had always seemed so independent, so modern, but now she only felt...sad. She could call Shelby, but her friend's answer to loneliness tended to be sex, and she would have wondered what Faith had done wrong to scare off Luke before she'd struck it rich.

Truth was, Faith didn't have any idea what she'd done wrong. Clearly she wasn't good at seducing men, but she'd never claimed to be good. She would have bet the bank that a man—being a slave to his penis of course—would have leapt at her offer of unencumbered physical relations.

Which didn't speak so well of her desirability.

Maybe what had happened tonight—or hadn't happened—was for the best. And honestly, had she really thought she could keep a big, sensual, earthy, edgy man such as Luke sexually satisfied?

Clearly, he'd done them both a favor by not showing up, he really had. Besides, now that she was thinking clearly, she remembered the truth about sex. It was like chocolate, fun in the moment but messy afterwards.

Yep, she was far better off without it.

With a pathetic sigh that didn't fool herself, she moved toward the desk and her stack of bills, determined to keep her chin up. Sure, yes, she'd rather be experiencing an orgasm beneath Luke's hands at this very moment, but that was life. She wouldn't waste time with regrets.

Besides, what she did here in the clinic was important to her, and deserved her time and thought. All she wanted, all she'd ever wanted, was to ease unnecessary suffering. She was doing that now, on a daily basis, and felt extremely proud of it.

And yet...she could admit here, alone with her bunny-slippered feet up on her desk, that maybe, just maybe, she was a little lonely because of it.

"Oh, get over yourself." She sat up straight and opened her bookkeeping program. She started flipping through the bills to figure out which ones she could pay now and which could wait.

Most went into the *wait* pile.

After only a few minutes of this, as the unpaid pile grew, her head started to swim. Damn it, she wasn't run down, she'd gotten her sleep...why would she be feeling these all-too-unwelcome symptoms of the virus now? Stress? The only stress she felt at the moment came from unfulfilled sexual urges, thank you very much Dr. Luke Walker, aka Dr. Universe, aka best kisser in the free world.

Looking for calm, she lit a few vanilla scented candles, her favorite, and practiced her breathing techniques for a few moments. And okay, maybe she stole a quick little bite of chocolate from her secret stash. Sue her.

Feeling better, she finished up sorting the bills, then sent the files to be paid to the printer. Now all she had to do was load the checks into the printer and she could hit the sack. Again. Sure, she'd have to hit it alone, but she was used to that, very used to it.

Unlocking her bottom drawer, she let out a rather unladylike oath when she saw she'd run out of checks. Figures. For a moment she let the overwhelming feeling of impending doom shake her. Help would be nice. An easing of the burden of running this place alone would be nice. Someone else keeping up the positive feelings for once would be *really* nice.

But she had her pride. Asking for help wasn't a part of her genetic makeup. Besides, who would she ask? Her employees already gave everything they had. Her family didn't have anything left to give. And there was no one else....

Luke, said a little voice, which she firmly ignored. She knew what he thought of this place, she knew he'd only come back out of a sense of duty. And guilt.

With another loud sigh, she pushed to her feet and headed out of her office. Naturally, the box of new checks was high on the shelf of the storage closet—the same one where Luke had turned her into one puddle of sexual urge earlier, but someone had moved the ladder she needed. She remembered seeing it in the staff room, and grumbling, she moved back down the hallway, still grumbling, into the staff room—

Whoa.

On the other side of the back door was a shadow of

a man. She grabbed the handy dandy, trusty baseball bat she kept in there to make her feel strong and brave, and hoisted it to her shoulder, squinting into the room, trying to figure out why that outline seemed so unbearably familiar— *"Luke?"*

His fist, raised and ready to knock, loosened, and he slowly, still staring at her, waggled his fingers.

Suddenly dizzy again, she put a hand to her head and tried to think. There was only one reason why he was standing there, and that reason had to do with her very bold, very brazen, rebel woman speech she'd given him earlier about having wild sex for two months and then walking away.

Now she stood there, fully lit by the staff room light in an oversize T-shirt with a rip over the collarbone and—oh my God—bunny slippers.

Oh yeah, utterly seductive sex siren. That was her.

7

LUKE DIDN'T KNOW WHAT had driven him back to Faith's. It was late, he was tired, and he had to be at the hospital at the crack of dawn.

Okay, he knew. Faith. She'd driven him here.

Since she simply stood on the other side of the door under the glow of the overhead light, staring at him like a deer caught in the headlights, he had to let out a low laugh directed fully at himself.

She'd changed her mind. Good. Great. At least one of them had come to their senses. But he hadn't taken two steps off the porch, toward his car, when the door whipped open behind him.

"Hi," she said breathlessly, pushing her long, glorious hair out of her face.

"Hi."

"You're just in time. I can't reach the box of checks, could you...?"

Then he was staring at her very fine ass because she'd grabbed his hand and was tugging him down the hall and back into the very storage room in which he'd nearly lost his mind with her earlier that day.

"I've got to tell you, Faith, this is becoming my favorite room in the place."

"There," she said, dropping his hand and pointing to a shelf high above him. "Could you...?"

But his gaze was locked on what she wore. Or on what she didn't wear. "Um...huh?"

"Oh, never mind." And right before his eyes, she started climbing the shelves.

Shamefully, it took him a long moment to stop her, but that's because he was busy absorbing the thin T-shirt that came to the tops of her thighs, a shirt that looked as if it had seen better days. The neckline, torn a little, left one creamy shoulder completely bare, the hem allowed him to gaze upon long, long, lean legs, all the way down to...her bunny slippers.

Then she got to his eye level and shot him a jaw-dropping view of white bikini panties with pink hearts on them.

"Forget you saw these," she said, still climbing.

He concentrated on not swallowing his tongue. "The bunny slippers or the hearts?"

"Oh, damn. Close your eyes!"

Yeah, right. He had them wide open. He'd never met a woman like her; so adorable he wanted to gobble her up, and so naturally, wildly sensual at the same time. "Faith, get back down here. I can—"

"Almost got them." She reached out, then her hand

wavered, in tune to the utter loss of color from her cheeks. "Oh, damn," she whispered again.

"Faith—" But she wasn't listening and she was going to fall, so he did what any man would have done, he wrapped his arms around her thighs, pressed his face to her butt and pulled her away from the shelves.

The box of checks came tumbling down.

So did the two of them, though Luke managed to cushion her fall for her—with his body.

"Ouch," he said from flat on his back, with her sprawled over top of him.

She turned over to face him. "You didn't have to play He-man. I told you, I almost had them."

"You were going to fall."

"No, I wasn't. At least not until you reminded me I was wearing bunny slippers."

"And panties with hearts on them," he pointed out.

Faith ignored that and wondered why it felt so good to be sprawled over top of him. "I should have just gotten the ladder myself. And worn heels. Then I could have reached the checks."

"What if you'd known I was coming? What would you have worn then?" Visions of lace and silk danced in his head.

"Armor."

Face-to-face, body-to-body, he lifted his head off the floor and searched her expression for a clue to her thoughts. "The bunnies are as much a turn on as the heels would have been."

She eyed him as if he were an alien.

He laughed with the woman he wanted to take to bed—a first. Feeling good, feeling sure of himself, he slid his hands down her body to her hips. "Really."

Her lips quirked as she studied his face. "You're a sick man, Luke Walker."

Tugging her a little off balance so that more of her was sprawled over more of him, he buried his face in her hair. "Did you mean it, Faith?"

"Did I mean what?"

Gently he lifted her head to look into her eyes. "About being together."

She didn't play coy and ask what that meant exactly. She knew. "I, uh, meant it at the time."

"At the time?"

"Yeah." She backed off him, sat cross-legged on the floor and clasped her fingers together, staring down at the chewed-to-the-quick nails. "Ever since I said it, I've been telling myself it was silly, you couldn't really want me. That I'd been too bold, that I'd scared you off. That you were afraid of me. Or didn't know how to reject me kindly. Or maybe—"

He shut her up with his mouth.

With a little squeak of surprise, then a moan of ac-quiescence that nearly killed him, she wrapped her arms around his neck and kissed him back. "Are we insane?" she asked.

"Without a doubt," he assured her, and leaned in.

Only to jerk back at the pounding on the clinic door. They both leapt to their feet.

"I'll get it," Luke said, pushing her behind him. "You stay here."

"Don't be ridiculous. This is my clinic, I'm going—"

"It's dangerous," he said, thinking of the hospital, and how they'd had a rash of crazy punks trying to get drugs from the lockup late at night. At least there they had an armed guard, but here Faith had no one to protect her. "Just let me go see—"

"No." She grabbed a doctor's white lab coat from a hanger and shrugged into it, covering that hot little bod except for those silly slippers. "Say another word about these slippers and you're dead meat."

And with that, she was gone.

WHEN FAITH SAW WHO WAS at the clinic door, she ran toward it, hauling it open. One of her patients, Ally Freestead, fell into her arms sobbing in relief.

"Oh, thank God," she cried. "I need to sit down."

No wonder, she was nine months pregnant. Faith looked around to grab a chair, but Luke was already there, supporting the now panting Ally.

"How long have you been having pains?" he asked,

putting his hand on her big belly and looking at his watch.

"Since the day I slept with the no good son-of-a-bitch who got me this way." Ally scrunched up her face and whimpered through the contraction.

"Hospital?" Luke asked Faith, seating Ally into a chair.

Ally panted. "No! I want Faith to deliver my baby here. Damn, this hurts! Give me a shot or something!"

Faith reached for her hand. "Do you remember the breathing exercises we've been doing?"

"Screw the exercises. I want drugs! Now! Oh God, now my legs are cramping, too!"

Faith dropped to her knees beside Ally and started rubbing her legs.

"Are those...bunny slippers?" Ally panted.

"You're hallucinating. Keep breathing," Faith said.

• *"Drugs!"* Ally screamed.

"Ally, you wanted to do this naturally, remember? Now if we just breathe together—"

"Faith—" Ally grunted through the last of the pain and let out a lusty breath of relief when the contraction passed. "I don't mean to be rude, but this sucks far worse than you said it would."

"I know, but we can do this—"

"Oh, God, here comes another!"

Luke looked at Faith and shook his head. "We need to get her into a room."

"No, don't move me!"

"Ally—"

"I have to push!"

AN HOUR LATER, ALLY was sleeping peacefully, and Luke was holding a squalling, red-faced, furious little boy who'd been brought into the world in less than fifteen minutes and two pushes.

A miracle, he thought, staring raptly down as the infant waved a fist wildly, his lungs in fine and full working order. "Who in the world are you so pissed at already?" he murmured, laughing softly when the infant hushed, startled, at the sound of Luke's voice.

"You okay?"

Turning, he found Faith in the doorway watching him. *Was he okay?* He'd just watched her, as he had over and over again now, get thoroughly engrossed in her work. She'd panted alongside Ally, sweated and laughed and cried with her as well, giving, as she always did, one hundred and ten percent to every single patient she had.

God, he loved that about her.

"Want me to take him?" she asked, holding her arms out for the baby.

"I'm fine. He just came out hungry."

"Ally wants to try to put him to her breast. I thought I'd check his diaper first—"

"I already did."

She blinked. "Really?"

"Aren't doctors allowed to do that?"

"Well, yes, but—"

He stroked the soft, downy head of the little boy who was slowly winding up for another temper tantrum. "Because in case you haven't noticed, this patient and I are having a deep discussion on life's meaning."

She laughed. "It's just that M.D.s don't usually—" At his raised eyebrow, she stopped. "Okay, I have to admit, you're not the typical doctor."

Now that caught his attention. "There's a 'typical' doctor?"

"Yeah, at least from a nurse's perspective there is. They're egotistical, arrogant, impolite...just to mention a few character flaws."

"I have all those traits," he said quietly. "Just ask anyone I've ever worked with."

"Well, you've worked with me," she said just as quietly, moving closer, her eyes on his face. "And I have to say, I don't see it."

"Are you forgetting what landed me here in the first place?"

"Maybe you've changed."

He stared at her, almost believing that. He hadn't realized there was anything wrong with his life before. Living for work had been all that mattered. Living for his patients.

But since he'd come here...

"You're the most compassionate man I've ever met," she whispered, putting her hand on his arm. "You're warm and giving, and—"

The infant in his arms let out one sharp howl, his eyes narrowed right on them. Then he opened his mouth, looking for all the world like a baby bird.

Faith laughed, and so did Luke, but his smile faded when he took a good long look at her. She was pale, and when she pushed a strand of hair from her face, her fingers shook slightly. With a frown, he reached out, stroked her jaw, and found her skin damp and clammy. "You okay?"

"Sure." But her smile wobbled and she didn't meet his eyes this time. "Just a long day."

Gently he bounced the baby, who was now crying, trying to soothe him as he kept his concentration on Faith. "After a long day, you yawn. You don't look like you're going to pass out." He stood up. "Sit down. Sit down," he repeated firmly when she weaved, and nudged her into the chair. "Faith—"

"It's probably just that stupid viral thing again," she said, leaning her head back, closing her eyes.

"When was the last time you had a physical?"

Her mouth tightened.

"Quite awhile, huh?"

"I'm fine."

"You're run down and something is off. Let me take a blood test."

"No."

"Faith—"

She curled up in the chair. "You want to be a good doctor? Then go take care of Ally while I catch five."

THE NEXT NIGHT FAITH was actually taking it easy. She wore sweat bottoms, a tank top and her beloved bunny slippers, and sat in front of the television doing as she so rarely did—nothing.

She'd done her accounting, and had shocked herself by being able to pay a few more bills than she'd expected. She'd placed her order for supplies and she'd gone over staff scheduling.

She was, in short, unaccustomedly caught up. At first, she hadn't known what to do with herself, but she'd figured it out soon enough between a bowl of homemade caramelized popcorn and the channel changer.

When the knock came at her door, she nearly leaped out of her skin in surprise. An emergency? No, if it was a clinic emergency, they'd be knocking downstairs, not on her door up here.

Now if she'd ordered that Chinese food she'd wanted...

Padding to the door, wishing she hadn't left her handy dandy baseball bat downstairs, she squinted through the window on the door.

That unbearably familiar shadow spoke for itself. So did the way her insides tingled and her nipples hardened.

Oh God, he'd finally come for that wild, unencumbered, animal sex she'd promised him! At just the thought, her thighs quivered. Damn, when would she learn? She needed to lounge around in silk and lace, not torn cotton.

A single soft, decisive knock sounded. "You going to let me in?"

Was she? A flash of them fulfilling her fantasies came to mind; both of them naked by moonlight, limbs tangled, rolling across her bed, breathless and hungry, devouring each other.

Oh yeah, she was going to let him in. She was going to let him—

"Open the door, Faith."

Yes, open the door, Faith. It took her a moment, mostly because her hands had gone a little slippery at the thought of him naked and willing, but she managed, probably with a far too needy expression on her face because he took one look at her and went utterly still.

Oh yeah, way to go, sexy momma. She patted her hair, which she had clipped up even though most of it had fallen back out. She tugged up the low-slung sweats that kept slipping, tugged down the thin tank top she'd washed so many times the pink had faded to light gray. "I'm sorry, I—"

"Stop." He put a hand on her arm to stop her fussing, then looked into her eyes. "You're so beautiful, Faith. I keep forgetting just how beautiful, then I see you and you take my breath."

By some miracle, she drew in some air. She might have laughed, but he wasn't laughing. Nope, his eyes were hot, hot, hot, and all that air she'd just dragged in got caught in her throat. "I—I didn't know you saw me that way."

"Then you're not paying attention."

"Luke—"

"Are you forgetting what it's like when we kiss?"

"Um...no."

"Good. Remember that, okay?"

Now she realized he was holding something behind his hands, looking at her...as if she was one of his patients.

"Let's sit down," he suggested. "What are you watching?"

He'd never taken an interest in anything as mundane as television, never. He'd certainly never been so...sweet. Narrowing her eyes, she held her ground. "Why are you suddenly using your best bedside manner on me?"

"What are you talking about? I'm always this charming."

When she just looked at him, he sighed. "Okay, truth..." He pulled his hands from behind his back. In them was a blood kit.

"No—"

"Yes." He slipped one of his big, warm hands in hers. "There's nothing to be afraid of, I'm actually really good at drawing blood—"

"I'm not afraid of a needle."

"Well, good, because I suspect you've got a problem with your blood sugar."

"I do not!"

"Look, Faith, humor me, okay? I know you think you've got that lingering flu virus—"

"I do—"

"But I think it's something else, and you can't just keep ignoring it, it's not safe."

What wasn't safe was how she'd actually thought he'd come here for another reason entirely, which was really humiliating when she dwelled on it, which of course she was. "I'll worry about myself."

"But that's silly. I'm right here and perfectly capable of getting those answers we need. We just get a little sample—"

She made an involuntary noise of angst and put her arms behind her back.

"It's just a finger prick."

What she really wanted was for him to vanish, to leave her alone with her fattening caramel popcorn and television set and overactive hormones, leave her alone to her very busy life which didn't have the room for a man. But before she could say so, he had her arm extended and resting on his thigh as he swabbed her finger with an alcohol pad.

"Okay, I lied. I don't like needles," she said, feeling absurdly nervous.

"Really," he said dryly.

Her heart was pounding, her palms sweaty. "Aren't you supposed to be distracting me?"

"If you're good, I'll give you a lollipop."

She tried not to tense. "You have a lollipop?"

"Well, no..." He flashed a grin. "Okay, pick another prize. Anything."

You, she thought inanely. *I pick you.*

"Can't think of anything?" He stroked her arm. "I've gotta admit, I'm a little surprised, Faith. You always seem to know exactly what you want. Don't hold your breath... Relax, just a small poke—"

"Ouch!" she yelped, but she didn't really mean it, it was more the anticipation that startled her than the actual pain. He was, as he'd promised, good at it.

She had a feeling he was good at everything he set his mind to. He was intent on what he was doing now, squeezing a drop of blood from her finger—

"Ouch!" she complained again.

"Big baby."

"I am not, I—"

"Shh." Head bent to his task, he carefully bandaged her finger, then worked the kit to get her blood sugar count.

If he turned out to be right, and she was hypo- or hyperglycemic, it was going to be more than a little embarrassing. Here she was, a health professional, ignoring her own health.

But of course he was wrong. She just was overly susceptible to the flu, she—

With a sweet gentleness that made her feel more weak than the needle had, he lifted her finger to his lips. "All better?" he murmured silkily, and she melted. Might have melted right into his lap if his kit hadn't suddenly beeped into the air, startling her.

He looked at the little machine and all sexy playfulness left his face as he let out a low, long whistle. "I suppose you're going to tell me it's the flu, not that caramel popcorn that sent your blood sugar rocketing to twice the normal count, right?"

8

THE NEXT DAY LUKE WAS still thinking about it. He'd come to care for Faith, more than he expected, and damn it, he worried. He worried the same as he worried about any patient.

Well, maybe not exactly the same.

She came to the lab at the hospital to get full blood work done. She was classified as borderline diabetic, which she could control by diet if she chose. She did.

He knew how Faith felt about natural healing, knew she'd follow proper diet, etc., get the proper exercise and that she would keep it all under control. Logically, he really did know this. She was smart, she was healthy, she knew what to do.

Which made the intense fear he felt for her way over the top. The urge to beat his chest and act all Neanderthal, insisting she let him help her, was horrifyingly strong.

Somehow he managed to rein it in, though when he went to her house the next night, she didn't answer the door. Fine. A clear message. He could deal with that.

On his next Saturday at the clinic, she played it cool.

So did he. He'd been e-mailing her all sorts of info regarding diabetes, which she'd been politely thanking him for. She wrote that she and Shelby had figured out a dietary plan to properly control her blood sugar and that she was fine, thank-you very much, and that she'd see him next Saturday.

No mention of hot sex, damn it.

Burying himself in his own hospital work helped. After one particularly brutal shift, he just happened to walk by the nurses' station, as he did a thousand times a day. Since he worked regularly with several of the women standing there, he nodded and smiled.

All talking abruptly stopped and they just stared at him.

He looked down to make sure he hadn't violated any social niceties, but his zipper was up and every button was in its place. "Uh...problem?"

One of the nurses let out a startled laugh. "No, you're...fine. I think."

"It's just that we've never seen you smile at us," said a dark-haired nurse whose name he was ashamed to admit he couldn't remember.

Had he truly never smiled at a nurse? Not once? "Are you sure?"

"Quite," said the third nurse, a tall, thin blond

woman who didn't look so eager to forgive as the first two.

He shook his head. "I must have—"

"Never," she said, and when he still was unconvinced, she lifted a challenging brow. "Okay, then... what's my name?"

He hated that he didn't know, hated even worse that smug see-told-ya smile she sent him. Damn, he really was a jerk.

The first nurse seemed to feel a little sorry for him. "I've been wanting to tell you, I think that clinic is really working for you. You seem to be...softening."

Softening? Luke started to frown but she leaned over the counter and patted his arm. "No, that's a good thing! Keep it up."

"And the smiling, too," the dark-haired one added. "That's a nice touch."

Then they waved at him, and duly dismissed, he started walking again.

This time as he went, he kept his gaze up, instead of on the files in his hands. The oddest thing happened— people made eye contact back. Most even smiled.

But it was the smile of one certain sexy redhead he couldn't stop thinking about as he walked outside toward his car. He'd been giving a lot of thought to her offer, the one that involved both of them being naked and panting, and wondered how it was they'd never actually gotten there. Women in labor and blood sugar problems and life in general kept getting in their way.

He wanted to rectify that. He was so intent on figuring out how to do just that, he figured he was dreaming when he saw her in the parking lot of the hospital, standing next to her car, kicking her back tire.

Her flat tire.

"Take that!" She kicked it again, then swore and hopped up and down in a circle, holding her toe.

Moving in, he reached for her arm to help balance her. "Did you break it?"

At the sight of him she let out a squeal, lost the rest of her balance, and fell against him.

Which really worked out in his favor, because once again he ended up with a curvy, warm armful of woman. Taking full advantage of that, he ran his hands down her slim spine, buried his face in her wild hair and closed his eyes, pretending she meant to be against him like this.

"Sorry," she murmured.

Because he couldn't help himself—she smelled so good, felt so good—he danced his mouth along the column of her throat. "Why?"

"Because—" This ended in a little whimper when he opened his mouth and took a little bite out of her.

Her hands fisted in the front of his shirt and she arched a little closer, letting out a soft, muffled groan when he did it again. "Luke—"

"You taste so good," he murmured. "So damn good. I've been thinking about this for weeks." And he let his mouth slide up, over her jaw to the very corner of her lips.

"Oh my," said a female voice behind them. "Excuse us..."

Luke looked up at the women, the nurses he'd just spoken to inside. They stood there, jaws open. "Good evening," he said.

"Evening," they said together, still staring. Then, as if they suddenly realized they were doing so, they jumped, looked at each other, and hurried off.

"My God, he's got a *girlfriend*," came back in an amazed whisper on the night air. "Maybe he *is* a nice guy."

Luke laughed softly and shook his head. "I really did have a PR problem."

"Did?"

He looked down into Faith's eyes. "Before you."

She wore a lacy, cream-colored tank top and a long, flowing, colorful gauzy skirt that flew around her ankles when she moved. He wanted to gobble her up whole. "Never mind," he said, hugging her. "How did you know what time I'd get off?"

"I didn't. I...came to see a patient."

Oh. Oh, yeah. Her universe didn't revolve around him. He laughed at himself—what else could he do?—and backed up a step, letting his hands fall to his sides. "Of course."

She bit her lower lip, looking so pretty by moonlight he had to put his hands in his pockets so they'd behave. "But seeing you is a bonus," she said.

"Right."

Her mouth curved, her eyes lit with teasing, which normally he'd enjoy since there wasn't a single person in his life who ever teased him—except for his brother Matt, but that was closer to torture than teasing.

"It is," she insisted. "The best bonus of the night, right after that sugar-free brownie I consumed for lunch."

"You've been avoiding me like the plague since I made you check your blood sugar, so don't talk to me of bonuses. And you'd better have made sure it was really sugar-free—sometimes those labels—"

"It *was*," she insisted. "And maybe I've been avoiding you because of embarrassment."

"Embarrassment? Why?"

With the teasing light out of her eyes now, she lifted her hands and let out a disparaging sound. "I'm supposedly a health professional. How does it look that I missed keeping track of my own health? I'm borderline diabetic for God's sake, and brushed it off as the flu."

"You've been busy."

"And stupid. *Stupid,*" she repeated when he opened his mouth to deny it. "And at the very least I owe you a thank-you."

"That, I'll take," he decided, his body quivering to hopeful attention when she stepped close and slid her hands up his chest. When she leaned in for a kiss, he wrapped her in his arms and prepared to be transported to heaven.

But after a short, sweet peck she pulled back.

"That's it?" he asked.

She let out a laugh at his disappointment. "I thought that was a very nice thank-you."

"Truthfully? I was hoping for nicer." He once again slipped his hands into his pockets. It was that or trace them over every inch of her. "So what happened to your tire?"

"I have no idea. I'll have to call AAA since I don't have a spare."

He pulled his cell phone from his pocket and handed it to her, listening as she argued with the dispatcher over the wait time.

"Have them tow it to your mechanic's place," he said. "I'll take you home."

When she handed him the phone back, he linked

their fingers. "Let's have dinner first." He nodded to the café across the street. "The food's guaranteed to clog your arteries, but it's delicious."

She looked at the café, then at him. "Dinner?"

"Dinner."

"As in...a date?"

Now he had to laugh. "Pretty tame given the sort of relationship you once proposed to me, don't you think?"

Now her green, green eyes darkened. "That other relationship that I proposed...I thought maybe we should just forget it."

"You thought wrong."

Her gaze dropped from his eyes to his mouth. "Really?"

"Really." She licked her bottom lip in an utterly unconsciously hungry gesture that nearly did him in. "Faith...don't do that unless we're skipping dinner and going straight to bed."

She did it again, sweeping her tongue over her lower lip.

He stepped close, put his hands on her hips.

She bit his lower lip.

"Okay," he groaned. "So you don't want dinner."

"Dinner means conversation." She very carefully arched a little closer so that his eyes crossed with lust. "Dinner means getting to know each other, but we've agreed, when you're done at the clinic, we're done. So getting to know each other will only lead to pain." Her hips hugged his. "I'm not interested in pain, Luke." Another subtle glide of those hips. "Not at all."

There was a very good reason why her words didn't make any sense to him, a reason having to do with maybe wanting more than just sex, but that couldn't be. All he'd ever wanted from a woman was a temporary, hot, good time. He might have tried to think that through, but she kept writhing against him, and with her wrapped around him like plastic wrap, his brain cells were malfunctioning left and right.

"Luke?" She looked at him with sleepy, sexy eyes. "Are you ready?"

His hands couldn't get enough of her, and he dipped down slightly to better align their bodies, which wrenched a groan from each of them. "Oh, yeah, I'm ready." The material of her tank top was thin enough that her nipples, hardened and pouting, were clearly defined. The sight nearly brought him to his knees. With one reverent finger he reached out and ran a finger over the scooped neckline. "But we're still going to eat first."

He insisted on that, no matter how much she protested. He took them both across the street and fed her while they waited for the tow truck. When she had food inside her and the tow truck had taken her car, he looked at her. "*Now*, Faith. My place. It's closer."

"Good." She got into his car. "How fast does this baby go?"

Somehow he gathered his wits and got them out of the parking lot. At the corner he stopped for a red light and then made the mistake of looking over at her.

She strained toward him, held back by the seat belt. Her eyes were lit with fire. The pulse at the base of her throat beat erratically. Her mouth was open, just a little, as if she had to have it open to breathe. Wayward strands of hair framed her face, and her nipples still pressed against her top.

She looked thoroughly tousled and ready for more ravaging. He closed his eyes and groaned. "You keep looking at me like that and we're not going to make it home."

"Luke."

He opened his eyes. Big mistake. She was smiling, and it was the very smile of sin. "I turn you on," she whispered, obviously empowered by the knowledge, which made him all the harder.

Shifting uncomfortably in his seat, he swore roughly, and when the light didn't change, he reached for her, held her face, slid his fingers into her glorious hair and lost himself in one of their patented long, wet kisses he could have happily drowned in.

"Oh," she breathed in helpless surprise when they came up for air. "Oh my."

She was sweet, so damned sweet he wanted to never let her go. "Faith—"

With a hungry murmur she unhooked her seat belt and plastered herself even closer, and he was lost. Again, he cupped her breast, and they both caught their breath. Her perfect, mouth-watering nipple poked hopefully into his palm, and he tugged gently at it with his fingers, making her whimper in pleasure, making him want to whimper, too. He tugged again and she shifted her thighs restlessly, making him ache to be between them.

God, she was soft and giving, and under his hands her flesh was warm and curvy. He couldn't get enough. He was afraid he could never get enough. Even with her hand settled possessively over his heart, her other doing its best to see him bald before he hit middle age, he needed more. Sliding one hand down the material of her skirt until he found smooth, sleek leg, he'd nearly honed in on heaven when a honk from behind them made them both jerk.

"Green light," she gasped with a breathless little laugh.

For a heartbeat he could only stare at her. It was painful, physically painful, to let her go, and for a moment he actually forgot how to drive, but another honk from behind them galvanized him into action and he managed to get them headed in the right direction.

At the next red light, she let out another breathless laugh and held up her hand when he reached for her. "We'll kill each other."

He slid his palm up her leg. "Yes, but that's the idea..." Her eyes were huge, her mouth swollen and thoroughly kissed free of any gloss. Her hair had rioted beneath his hungry fingers, clinging to her cheek, jaw and throat in a thick, curly mass that made him want to sink back into her. "My God, you take my breath away."

Her eyes lit, and as she had before, she fisted her hands in his shirt and hauled him close, putting her mouth to his. "Drive," she said when she pulled back. She smiled into his eyes and let out a slow breath. "Drive fast."

"Driving fast," he muttered and put the car in gear. "Driving really fast."

9

By some miracle they made it to Luke's house without another red light. He leapt out of the car, came around for Faith, and tugged her out and into his arms.

After another long, breathless kiss, he pulled back and ran a finger over her wet lower lip. "I love your mouth. I can't get enough of it."

She'd never had a man say such things to her, never. It spun her head, and that, she figured a little recklessly, shamelessly, was okay. For the next month and a half, this man and all the wild sexuality that rolled off him in waves, belonged to her.

"Come on," he whispered, and led her to his front door. While he fumbled for the right key, looking adorably flustered and hot and just a little frustrated, she smiled and rimmed his ear with her finger.

He dropped his keys, swore, then bent for them. When he straightened, he snagged an arm snug around her, pinning her arms to her sides so he could get them into his house.

She leaned in and sucked on the lobe of his ear.

"Stop that," he gasped. Kicking the door shut behind them, he planted her against the wood and let out a groaning laugh at her feigned docile expression. "Okay, don't stop anything, but I can't be held responsible if you drive me so crazy we don't make it to the bed."

Her heart was drumming so fast and loud it was a miracle it didn't burst right out of her chest. Holding his gaze, she leaned over and slowly, purposely, bit his lower lip.

With a groan, he captured her mouth in a kiss so carnal and fierce, Faith thought she might spontaneously combust right there on the spot. He had her pressed up against the door, his mouth on hers, kissing her as if he was a man dying of thirst.

She'd once wondered what would happen when he lost control, and she was about to find out. Knowing that she'd done that to him, driven him over the edge, swamped her. Power and need swept through her, power and a need so crippling her legs buckled.

He caught her, his mouth still on hers, his hands running wildly over her body. Then, holding her head, he raised his mouth from hers a fraction and stared down, his eyes blazing. He stared into her eyes, then down at her lips, before changing the angle of her head and settling his mouth over hers again. When she danced her tongue to his, he groaned deep in his throat, the sound fueling the fire within her.

"Oh, my...Luke—"

"Yeah." His fingers left her hair, sweeping down her body, over her breasts, and she nearly cried. *Now*, she thought, now he'd give her relief from the wild, desperate need flooding through her. "Luke...please."

"I know. I know." His thumbs rasped over her nipples and she did cry out, covering his hands with hers, holding them over her aching breasts. He groaned again, but managed to disengage his fingers from her, leaving her nearly sobbing in frustration.

But those talented, greedy hands didn't leave her entirely. They slid down, down her body until his rough fingertips got to about mid-thigh. Then, holding her gaze, he started bunching up the hem of her skirt, crushing it in the palm of his hands until his fingers brushed against bare skin. Still looking into her eyes, he slid his hands beneath her panties and cupped her bottom. His fingers squeezed, dug in, and then he hauled her up so she could wrap her legs around his hips.

That left the hottest, wettest, neediest part of her nudging the most impressive erection she'd ever imagined. With a moan low in her throat, she slid her fingers into his hair and thunked her head back against the door as he slowly rocked against her in a rhythm as old as time.

Leaning in, he kissed her throat, her collarbone, her breast through her tank top. "Lift it," he demanded hoarsely, and groaned when she did just that, watching her fingers intently as she brushed them over her own flesh.

"Like this?" She exposed her pale pink bra, gasping as he continued to slowly thrust his sex against the damp, hot place at the apex of her thighs.

"Oh, yeah, like that." Another aching thrust. "Open your bra, Faith."

Obeying, she unhooked the latch in front and looked into his fiery eyes.

"More," he said, "all of it," and she slowly peeled it open.

There was something incredibly erotic, astonishingly intimate about having his hands holding her thighs open to his, having his hips moving against her in a slow, tight, rocking motion, in a perfect imitation of what she really wanted him to be doing to her, all while she undressed herself to his hungry, hot gaze.

Bending his head, he reverently stroked his cheek against her bared breast, then opened his mouth and captured it, taking a gentle bite that he promptly soothed with a stroke of his tongue before he sucked her into his mouth, hard.

Her world spun out of control, centered on the sensation bombarding her between her legs and what he was doing to her now with his mouth. Then abruptly, he let her go, wrenching a whimper from her.

"Yeah, it's good isn't it..." He slowly blew out a breath over her tight, wet nipple, coaxing the bud into an even tighter peak.

"Oh, please," she whispered, arching against him, helping him by meeting him thrust for thrust. Her toes curled, her fingers fisted tighter in his hair as she arched into him, so close, so desperately close, she saw stars, she heard bells, she—

"Faith? Your skirt is ringing."

She stared at him, dazed, as the truth sank in. Her phone really was ringing and with a look of searing frustration, he slowly let her legs slide down his body so she could stand.

"No." She wanted to stomp her foot, scream in frustration. "Shelby's supposed to be on call."

"It looks like maybe that got changed."

"Do you believe Fate's laughing at us?"

"No, I don't believe in fate, not like that. We make our own destiny, and Faith? We will do this."

"Just not now."

He sighed and put his forehead to hers. "Just not now."

LUKE WAS FIT TO BE TIED as he glared at Carmen, who sat on a cot in one of the patient rooms at Faith's clinic. "You did *what* to pop your stitches?"

They'd driven over here after talking to Shelby, who had gotten stuck at home with a sick mom and couldn't come in.

Which meant Luke had been forced to take his hands out of Faith's very lovely pink panties and his mouth off her heart-stopping nipples, and be grown up about yet another interruption keeping him from what he knew would be an explosive orgasm with Faith.

He still couldn't walk straight.

Lifting her chin in the air, Carmen sniffed.

"Don't yell at my patient." Faith came back into the room with a tray of equipment. "I'm sure she didn't mean to rip the stitches."

Carmen erupted into a tirade in Spanish, complete with wild hand gestures.

"English!" Luke demanded.

She crossed her arms over her chest. "I unwrapped the bandages to scratch, then forgot to wrap it back up. I accidentally reached out to grab a cup that was falling and stretched too far. *Okay?*"

"Okay," Faith said gently, stepping between them. "But you ripped open the wound. You need to be re-stitched."

Luke sighed. Faith's mouth still looked full and puffy from all the kissing they'd done. She was all straightened and refastened now, but he couldn't look at her without remembering how she'd looked peeling her bra away from her breasts.

"I want *her* to do it." She jerked her bleeding thumb at Faith.

"That's fine," Faith said soothingly. "And this time, you'll be more careful. *Si?*"

Carmen's lips twitched. "You speak Spanish now?"

"*Un poca.*"

"*Poco,*" Carmen corrected and smiled. "I like you."

Luke tossed up his hands and turned in a slow frustrated circle.

"I must have interrupted something good, eh? I'm sorry."

Luke sighed again, loudly.

"Whoa—" Carmen blanched when Faith lifted a suturing needle, "Not again."

"Trust me," Luke said grimly. "You're going to have to drug her."

"Yes, drugs," Carmen agreed.

"It's not going to be that bad," Faith said, but no matter how she coaxed and cajoled, Carmen insisted on meds.

Within five minutes she was high as a kite. "Ooh, I feel good." Carmen eyed Luke. "Bet you wish you didn't have to take me home again." She cackled and

laid back, beaming drunkenly at the ceiling. "Just remember, kiddies, abstinence makes the heart grow
fonder."

Luke just groaned.

"I WAS JUST KIDDING about the abstinence thing," Carmen whispered groggily, her head lolling on Luke's
head as he carried her from his car to inside his house.
"I mean, sometimes I like to bring you down a peg or
two, but I really do love you and want you to be
happy."

He set her down on one of his spare beds and
sighed. "I know."

"And I was just kidding about not liking you," she
murmured, snuggling into the covers.

"I know." He tossed a blanket over her. "And you
didn't know you'd be allergic to the pain meds I gave
you."

"That's right." She opened her sleepy eyes briefly.
"It's all your fault. Faith didn't think I needed any
drugs."

Luke sighed, shook his head. "Go to sleep, damn it,
before I strangle you."

"I'm sorry my sister wasn't here to watch me."

"Yeah. Me, too." He made it to the door before she
called him again. "What now?"

"She's really wonderful, you know. I couldn't have wished for anyone better than her for you." She narrowed her eyes and lifted her bandaged hand to point at him. "So don't blow it. Got it?"

"Say good night, Carmen."

"Good night, Carmen." Still grinning, she closed her eyes.

ALONE IN HER BED, more than a little hot and bothered, Faith let out a careful breath and stared at the shadows on the wall.

She could have gone with Luke and Carmen.

If she had, she'd be in his great, big, warm bed right this very minute.

With Carmen just down the hall.

Not sure about her ability to remain quiet if Luke touched her again—after all, he'd had her sobbing his name with only his mouth on her breast—she figured she'd have to wait for another opportunity. An opportunity without an audience or chance of interruption.

Waiting shouldn't be so hard, but at the clinic tonight, watching them leave, she'd thought it just might kill her.

She could admit now, most of that had been pure lust. It'd taken over her every movement, her thoughts and especially her senses.

She'd already decided there was nothing wrong

with that once in a while. Nothing wrong with a good bout of mutually satisfying sex.

So now why did she ache at the thought of it being just sex and nothing more? Why did she suddenly worry about being with a man who didn't love her, and might never love her?

Because she was starting to fall, that's why. She'd really started to fall.

And she was just old-fashioned enough to feel that if she had to fall, then damn it, so did he.

10

THE WEEK FLEW BY. Faith had a meeting one night with her staff—okay, it was pizza night, not a meeting. Another night, she and Shelby caught a movie. She spent one night alone at the library reading for pleasure, something she told herself she didn't get enough of, and one night doing her least favorite chore of food shopping, which, given her new status as borderline diabetic, had become a bigger chore than usual since she had to completely avoid the candy aisle.

Managing her blood sugar level was more time-consuming and far more difficult than she'd have ever imagined. And even with all the time she devoted to it, there were still times she couldn't get it right and had to deal with the annoying bouts of dizziness and tiredness in spite of her best efforts.

The flu would have been far more preferable.

As to why she avoided Luke—and she was avoiding him—bottom line, a morbid sense of impending pain. Not physical, but the kind that was worse. Heartache kind of pain.

On Saturday, Luke showed up at the clinic, and if

he'd noticed she'd made herself scarce, he didn't say a word. He worked hard and long beside her and her staff, but didn't attempt to get her into the storage closet, didn't even attempt to seek her out in any way at all.

Had he changed his mind, too? And why was that not okay with her?

Later that night, long after everyone had left, she climbed into her bathtub piled high with steaming water and jasmine-scented bubbles. Probably the sensual scent hadn't been the wisest choice, but she sank deeply and sighed deeply.

Right now there was only one thing that could possibly improve the night—well, two. Chocolate.

And Luke.

But neither was going to happen for her.

When the doorbell rang, her heart jerked. Steeped in bubbles, she went still, but the bell ran again. With water splashing everywhere, and a good amount of bubbles, too, she got out of the tub and wrapped herself in a towel. Dripping her way to the door, she held her towel to her breasts and took a calming breath. Then she flipped on the outside light.

Luke stood there. At the sight of him, her pulse kicked into overdrive. Surely the people in the next building could hear her heart pumping. Stepping closer to the glass, she put her hand on the wood, as if she could touch him. Wanting snaked through her, wanting, and that terrible ache, all at the same time.

He was standing close to the door, too, and suddenly she didn't want that barrier between them, so she pulled it open enough for him to move inside but turned her back to him, head bowed, knowing if she so much as looked at him, he'd see everything she felt, her need, her hope, her confusion—

From behind her, his fingers brushed the back of her hair, so light she might have imagined it, except he did it again. Then he bent his head, just enough to rub his jaw to hers. "Do you want me to go?"

So solemn. So quiet. So impossibly sexy.

"Faith?"

She closed her eyes, shook her head no. She didn't want him to go. She just didn't want him to see what she was thinking, or he'd run like hell.

He danced a finger down her bare, damp arm, letting out a shaky breath so close to her ear it drew goose bumps to her skin. "I got you out of the bath."

Since the air had backed up in her lungs at his touch, at the way his chest spread heat across her back, how the front of his thighs brushed the back of hers, she could only nod.

"I don't want to talk you into this," he whispered, tingling his fingers over her shoulder, playing with the edging of the towel at her shoulder blade.

Turning to face him, she pressed her hands flat against the door behind her to keep them off him. "It was my idea to begin with."

"Yeah." He smiled, a slightly unsure smile that touched her more than anything else he'd ever done. "So why do I get the feeling you've changed your mind?"

She had changed her mind, she'd deepened it. No longer was wild sex on weekend nights for the time they had left going to be enough for her, but how to admit that to a man who gave commitments only to his patients? She couldn't explain, it was that simple. It would be her own secret joy...and loss. "I still want you," she whispered.

His eyes heated at that, and keeping his eyes on hers, he pulled his pager out of his pocket and tossed it over his shoulder on to her couch.

She watched it bounce on the cushion, then turned her gaze back to him. He was dangling his cell phone from his fingers. It, too, took a sail across the room, landing next to his pager.

She took a few steps to where her portable phone sat on its base. She hit the talk button in tune to Luke's raised brow. Her pager sat next to the phone and she carried both to the couch and slid them beneath the cushion. After a very brief consideration, she slid his pager and cell phone beneath the cushion as well.

He grinned.

So did she, grinned as she stepped right into his arms.

"I've never laughed while getting a woman naked before," he admitted, and nibbled at her throat.

With a little moan, she tilted her head to give him better access. "You're not going to have to work very hard to get me naked."

He eyed her towel. "No?"

"No." She untucked the edge of the towel, and let it fall.

Luke sucked in a sharp breath, his eyes flaming, his hands shaking slightly as he peeled himself out of his shirt and sent it the way of his pager and phone.

Wide shoulders, broad chest, ropey arms...did he know how mouth-watering he was? His torso was lightly spattered with dark silky hair, across his tight pectorals, in a line dividing his flat, corded belly, disappearing into the pants that seemed quite strained across an impressive bulge behind his zipper.

"I'm still ahead of you," she said softly, standing there completely nude except for the few drops of water left from her bath.

"Yeah." His voice sounded strained, rough, and he kicked off his shoes and socks, unfastened his pants, grimacing as he slid them down over his erection.

"Oh my," she whispered, unable to tear her gaze

away, but she hadn't seen a man up front and personal in so long, had in fact *never* seen such a magnificent—

With a groaning laugh, he surrounded her with his warm, strong arms, lifting her up.

She licked her lips and studied his mouth. "Are we going to—"

"Yes."

"In my bedroom?"

"Yes."

"All the way to the end this time?"

"Definitely, yes. Any more questions?"

"Yes. Could you hurry?"

"Maybe the first time, but definitely not the second time. Or the third."

When her mouth fell open as he walked with her down the hall, he let out another groaning laugh. "I want you in a bed, Faith. Sprawled out so I can touch and kiss and lick every single inch of you."

He was going to touch and kiss and lick every inch of her. Thank God. He was going to do that because she'd asked him to, because she'd told him it was what she wanted, and she did want it, so badly she was trembling in anticipation, but she also wanted much, much more—

Bending, he rubbed his jaw with hers, tenderly, sweetly, and gently laid her down on her bed, making her forget everything but him. With his finger, he leaned over her and smoothed the furrow she got between her eyes when she thought too much. "Uh-oh," he whispered. "You're looking tense." With a knee on the bed and his wide palms on her shins, he ran them up her legs. "Can't have that."

His hands slid over her knees and kept going, and her heart started that heavy drumming again.

"Cold?" he murmured. He'd reached her thighs. She managed to shake her head.

"Good." Sliding his hands around the back of her thighs now, he pulled them open, then looked down at what he'd exposed, and let out a low, rough, serrated breath.

So did she.

His hands were on the move again, over her legs, fingers outstretched...until they almost reached...the apex of her thighs. Now it was her turn to suck in a breath, her hips arching toward him, waiting, desperately waiting. Then he touched, and she cried out.

"You're so beautiful, so perfect." Carefully, slowly, he bent his head...

She felt his warm breath brush over her and went utterly still, suddenly a little unsure. "Um...Luke—"

"Shh..."

"But—" At the first touch of his tongue she nearly exploded.

At the second touch she did.

Brilliant lights, blood roaring in her ears, skin too tight for her body, heart threatening to burst out of her chest, the whole enchilada as she came wildly, helplessly.

And came. And came.

Finally, after what might have been two seconds or two hours, she was flat on her back, blinking at the ceiling, fists in the sheets, legs held open by Luke's wide shoulders.

He lifted his head from where he'd been kissing her inner thigh. "You okay?"

She considered. "I can't feel my toes."

He lifted up a little. "Better?"

"No."

His face fell, and she nearly laughed, but this was not a laughing matter. "Do you want to know what would make it all better?" she whispered.

He didn't look sure, and she nearly laughed again because how often did she get to see Dr. Universe look unsure? "What would be better," she said, "is you inside me."

His smile was slow and wide and stopped her heart. Then he gave her what she wanted, he was inside her, and her heart started up again in a slow, heavy beat because nothing, nothing, had ever felt so right.

"Faith." He cupped her face and leaned in to kiss

her as he slowly withdrew, his hot, hard length dragging on her hot, wet flesh, and just when she started to whimper in protest, he came back with one long thrust. Then another. And another, and she felt that tight, unbearable, anticipation build back up.

"Again," he urged against her mouth. "Come for me again, Faith." And to ensure she did just that, he slid a hand between them, cupped a breast and stroked her nipple with a slightly rough thumb.

Gasping, she arched into him.

"That's it..." His hand skimmed over her quivering belly now, down, down, until his thumb could help keep up the rhythm in the wet curls between her legs, all while he urged her on with soft, sexy words no man had ever uttered to her before.

Fingernails embedded in his butt, head tossed back, dark and needy noises being ripped from her throat, she came completely undone for him. Again. Vaguely she heard him lose control, too, with a rough, guttural groan and her name on his lips as he sank over her hot, damp, replete body.

Dazed, she held him to her, drowning in pleasure, drowning in him.

Unbelievably, she started to doze...all the way up until she realized they hadn't given a single thought to birth control.

Some health professionals they were.

A FEW MINUTES LATER, Luke got the bum's rush out Faith's door. On the porch in the cool night air, he turned to her just as she shoved his jacket in his hands and shut the door on him. "Faith—"

She opened it a crack. "I've got to get up early."

"Yeah." But that wasn't the issue and he knew it. He could tell by her glossy eyes and pale skin she was just as blown away as he was—hell, make that terrified—by what had just happened, by how they'd so completely lost it. "Faith, we didn't use birth control."

She let out a shrill laugh, then covered her mouth.

"You noticed," he said, then scrubbed his face with his hands. "I've never forgotten before. Christ, I'm so sorry. I swear to you, you won't catch anything—"

Another half-hysterical laugh escaped her mouth and with a sigh he pushed the door all the way open and gathered her resisting body close. "If it's a pregnancy you're worried about, we'll deal with it. Together. Okay?"

She didn't answer so he pulled back to see her face. "Faith. We face it together."

She dropped her hand away from her mouth. "We're *professionals*. I see the effects of teens not using birth control every single day— My God, I coach them all the time on the importance of abstinence, and what do I do? I get so completely carried away—"

"*We*," he interrupted. "It was a *we* thing tonight in the carried away department."

"You know what I mean."

"Yeah." And there was no excuse, none.

"I mean, we even planned this," she said, baffled. "I even purchased—" Breaking off, she blushed.

"I did, too." He patted his back pocket. "Maybe I should pin them to my shorts next time."

She bit her lip. Glanced up at him. "Next time?"

"Isn't there going to be a next time?" Please, God, let there be a next time.

"But we were so stupid about it."

"We won't ever be again," he vowed, so shockingly close to begging he had to forcibly close his mouth.

"There's five weeks left," she said very softly.

"I want every one of them."

"That's what I promised you. But...for the rest of tonight I think I'd like to be alone."

Suddenly he wished he'd negotiated the *sleeping* part, too. It'd have been nice to stay with her curled in his arms all night long.

And while he was at it, he should have negotiated for more everything, since unlike all of his other sexual escapades—of which there hadn't been as many as he'd liked to think—he wanted more. Lots more.

"Good night, Luke."

He wished he could see her face, but she'd stepped

into the shadows. Apparently he was the only one here dwelling over their decision. Not good. Not good at all. "Good night, Faith."

FAITH DIDN'T KNOW WHAT she expected the next night. She got out of the bath and put on a robe as she thought about it. Would Luke come, even though it was a weeknight?

Or would he wait until the next weekend, until after they'd worked together all day? Certainly the weekend would be more convenient for him, because she imagined his busy schedule wouldn't permit him much of a personal life on the weekdays, plus certainly he wouldn't want to see her again so soon—

Her doorbell rang and she nearly swallowed her tongue.

Oh God. He'd come.

No. No, it couldn't be Luke, he'd just seen her yesterday, surely he wouldn't want to...

The surge of hope and joy that whipped through her was nothing short of pathetic.

But it turned out to be Shelby, dressed to the nines in a little black cocktail dress and heels, her blond hair artfully piled on top of her head. She held a casserole dish. "Here," she said. "I made extra. High on the protein, no sugar."

Faith took the delicious-smelling dish. "You cooked for me in that?"

"No, I cooked for my date." She let out a wicked grin. "He's getting a casserole dish, too, but for him, I also made dessert."

"Hey, I want dessert."

"His comes in black silk," she said with a low, throaty laugh. "So you'll have to make up your own—" Breaking off, she glanced over her shoulder at the sound of someone coming up the stairs. Her smile turned speculative as Luke came into view. "Well, look at that...you might get your own dessert after all."

Luke lifted a brow at that comment. He wore black as well, but not silk; black jeans, a black T-shirt, and in the moonlight looked tall, dark and devastatingly handsome.

"Dr. Walker..." Shelby turned back to Faith and jerked her eyebrows so high they disappeared into her hair. "Just what Faith ordered." With a laugh at her own inside joke, she leaned close to Faith and kissed her on the cheek. "I'd say have a good evening, sweetie, but I can see that you most definitely will. Nightie, night. Don't do anything I wouldn't do now...well, on second thought, there's nothing I wouldn't do, so have at it."

Faith listened to Shelby's heels clicking as she

walked off into the night, her heart starting a heavy beat of anticipation.

"That smells good," Luke said into the silence, gesturing to the casserole she held. "You going to share?"

She eyed him. "You didn't come over here to eat."

"No, but we're going to."

"My blood sugar is fine at the moment."

"Good. After we eat, I'm going to remove every stitch of clothing you're wearing."

He said it so conversationally, it took the words a moment to sink in. Once they did, her heart kicked into an even higher gear.

"And then...I'm going to make you wild."

"Awfully cocky," she managed evenly though her thighs tightened. So did her nipples.

"Yeah. I'm going to make you scream, too," He said this softly, silkily, and stepped even closer, still not touching her in any way.

And still her pulse doubled.

Tripled.

"I'm, um, not really much of a screamer," she said, quite proud of the fact her voice hardly quivered at all, though she was having a huge amount of trouble breathing and her knees had liquefied.

Holding her gaze prisoner, he took advantage of the fact that her hands were full of the hot casserole dish and tugged on her robe, completely exposing one bare breast.

Her gasp echoed around them.

"Mmm," rumbled from his throat. Then one big warm hand cupped the fullness, plumping it up for his seeking mouth, which was warm and greedy.

Staggering back a step, she hit the doorway.

"Hold on to our dinner now," he said around his mouthful, and using his teeth, gently plucked at her nipple. "Still got a grip on it, Faith?"

She whimpered and locked her knees together to keep from falling.

"Faith?"

"Y-yes."

"That's a girl."

And he locked the door behind them, after which he proceeded to make good on his promise to remove every stitch she wore, make her wild...and make her scream.

11

FOR THE NEXT FEW WEEKS Luke raced through his days at the hospital, enjoying his work as much as ever.

And enjoying his time off more than ever.

In the physicians' lounge after a particularly long shift, he gathered his things, shoveling them into his duffel bag, his mind already racing to the night ahead.

He thought he'd take Faith out for dinner, then planned on a delectable dessert by moonlight—*Faith* by moonlight.

"You out of here, Dr. Walker?"

Luke shouldered his bag and turned to face Dr. Nicole Mann, one of the youngest and most acclaimed new doctors they had. "That I am."

She was dark-haired and petite, and incredibly dedicated to her job at the hospital, specifically working for him in the E.R. The day Luke had been "sentenced" to work at the clinic, she'd come by his office—the only one to do so—offering her sympathy. She, more than anyone here on staff, understood his passion, and felt it as her own.

"You seem...lighter on your feet these days." She

tilted her head, studying him for a moment with a little smile touching her mouth. "And, dare I say it, even happy. You get another promotion I didn't hear about?"

"No."

"You done working at Healing Waters?"

"No."

"Well, then." She smiled expectantly. "What's your secret?"

Faith, he nearly said, and bit his tongue. She wasn't what was making him feel like dancing down the hospital hallways. Nope, it was...

Ah, hell.

It was Faith.

"Maybe it's because you have only three weeks left at the clinic."

Three weeks and then no more steaming hot, unbearably erotic rendezvous with Faith?

And suddenly he wondered why he'd ever agreed to that stupid time line. Why had he ever imagined it would be enough?

"I bet you'll be thrilled to get away from all those froufrou oils and self-healing crap, and come back to the scientific basics."

"Actually, the alternative therapies Healing Waters utilizes have been around for centuries," he said. "Longer than our scientific methods—" He broke off and stared at her, horrified at himself.

Had he just...defended alternative healing practices?

Dr. Mann looked just as shocked. "Yes...well, good night, Dr. Walker." Fast as she could, she hightailed it away from him.

Because, clearly, he was crazy. He'd have hightailed it away from himself, too.

Good God, what was happening to him? All his sexual affairs ended sooner or later, and he'd always been fine with that.

Maybe it was because they were impatiently waiting for Faith to get her period. She claimed to be completely irregular, often going two months in between, but he wanted to be sure. He couldn't just walk away until he was certain that there were no ramifications from their oversight. Surely Faith would know before his time was up.

Then, definitely then, he'd be ready to move on.

He left the hospital. And though he'd been looking forward to dragging Faith into his arms, he turned toward the beach instead, and went home. He didn't need to see her every single day. Nope, he sure didn't.

Undoubtedly she'd be grateful for the night off. After all, soon enough—in three weeks—they wouldn't be seeing each other at all.

LUKE DIDN'T COME TO HER that night. Or the next.

And by Saturday, Faith wasn't sure what to think,

except that she'd gotten way too dependent on his warm, strong arms, his melting smile, the way he made her feel.

She'd made a deal with him, a deal that was nearly over, and given his lack of appearances this week, it might already be over, and she would live with it.

Immersing herself in opening the clinic for the day, she was behind her desk going over the schedule when Luke walked in.

"Morning," he said.

Her heart had taken off before she even lifted her head from the schedule. He stood in the doorway already wearing his white coat over dark blue trousers that fit his long, powerful legs. Her head swam at just the sight of him, so she hoped he'd stay far, far out of her way for the day or surely she'd give herself away by drooling.

"Morning." Scooping up the schedule, she rose and walked around her desk, figuring she'd just walk right on by—without looking directly at him, because it was like looking directly into the sun, it was hazardous to her health—and go on with her day. Only *she* would know everything within her trembled to reach out for him. Only *she* would know she strained her nose to catch at least a little scent of him—

"Hey." His big, warm hand settled gently on her arm, stalling her retreat.

She studied his shoes. Nice ones. She wondered if his socks matched. Probably they did, since he was always so organized—

"Faith?" Bending slightly, he tried to peer into her eyes, and when she wouldn't let him, he captured her chin and slowly raised her face. "You're not okay."

He could see that? Well, wasn't that just fine and dandy. She spent a lot of effort trying to look like she felt perfectly fine even if her heart hurt. Come to think of it, her head hurt too. And damn if she wasn't just the slightest bit light-headed. "Of course I'm okay. We're busy today, so I'll just—"

"Did you eat breakfast?"

"I've told you, I can handle this thing."

"You need a snack?"

"I have a bagel on my desk. I'm going to get to it, I—"

"Get to it now." His thumb rasped over her lower lip, setting off a whole set of reactions in her body. "You're pale."

"Fine." Tossing the schedule down, she picked up the bagel and stuffed a bite in her mouth. "Happy?"

"I will be." He waited until she'd swallowed. "More." He looked at his watch. After sixty seconds, he lifted his head. "Feel better?"

"Yes," she admitted, and found her throat tight.

"Faith, sometimes you'll be off just because. It's not your fault."

At the sympathy in his gaze, she nearly burst into tears.

"I want you to go on insulin."

That dried her up. "No." She was standing her ground on this. "Insulin isn't the answer for me."

"Because it's *conventional?*"

"I'm going to overlook that sarcastic and uncalled-for comment because I can see you're worried about me, but—"

"Damn-A-straight I'm worried about you." He pulled her close. "I think about you all the time."

"Really?" Because she couldn't handle the heat, the concern, the devastating affection in his gaze, she turned her back to him and crossed her arms over her chest. "Because you didn't come over last night. Or the night before." Or the night before, but who was counting?

"Faith—"

"Forget it." She covered her eyes with her fingers. "I didn't mean to say that, didn't mean to sound like a nagging wife. We talked about this, it's a casual sex thing, nothing else—" She gasped when he whipped her around.

She expected anger, or more frustration, not the

sadness. "I stayed away from you," he said, "because yes, we agreed this was a casual thing, a weekend thing, an over-in-a-few months thing, and while I said it, agreed to it, I found myself..." He grimaced. "Look, just know that you're not the only one having trouble with this, okay? But it's all I have to offer you for now." His eyes were devastatingly regretful.

She swallowed hard past the lump in her throat. "I knew that up front."

"I don't do hard-core relationships, I—"

"I understand, Luke."

"I give everything to my work, which leaves nothing else—"

"I said I understand," she repeated softly.

He stared at her, then winced and closed his eyes. "But how can you, when I don't?"

"I just do. We're really very much the same. I give everything to my work, too, and often..." She lifted a shoulder. "There's nothing left. In the long run, you and I would burn out, I know that much. We wouldn't give enough to each other, we couldn't give it, that's just a fact."

Eyes solemn, mouth grim, he reached out and stroked her jaw. "Only a few weeks left," he whispered.

Unable to talk, she turned her cheek into his palm

and sighed. "So maybe we should make the most of it."

"Yeah." His mouth came down on hers, and because her eyes were still closed, it made her dizzy, a good dizzy this time, so she flung her arms around his neck and let it take her.

"Tonight?" she gasped when they came up for air.

His hair was wild from her fingers, his eyes, hot, hot, hot. "Tonight." Lowering his mouth, he feasted on her throat, her shoulder.

At a knock on her office door, they breathlessly broke apart.

"Faith?" called Shelby. "Is Dr. Walker in there with you? We could use him in room three."

Faith looked at Luke. "He's coming."

"Am I?" he murmured with a wicked smile.

"You will tonight," she murmured back, soaking up his low laugh.

Oh, yes, he was going to break her heart, and oh yes, she wanted him anyway. If this was all she could have, well, then, she wasn't going to waste a second of it.

It was a cruel joke that she couldn't seem to get sated, that she always needed more, but she'd deal with that, too, when the time came. But for now, she was going to smile.

"Tonight then," he whispered, and with one last hard kiss, he was gone.

ONE DAY THE NEXT WEEK, Luke staggered into the hospital, his body still humming from the night he'd spent with Faith. He'd just had the hottest, steamiest shower of his life, and it had nothing at all to do with the water temperature, but the fact Faith had joined him with a naughty smile and a handful of soap.

He wondered if anyone could read what his idiotic grin meant, and attempted to swipe it off with darker, somber thoughts of work, but he couldn't.

He practically danced down the hospital hallways. Passing the nurses' station, still smiling, he waved.

Clearly still a little cautious of him, they waved back.

One week left.

Ah, there it was. A thought that managed to dim his smile. Only one week.

Briefly he considered making another stupid comment to the press about the clinic, one which would guarantee the need to spend another three months there. But since he couldn't even remember how or why he'd felt so strongly against it in the first place, and since it would only hurt Faith anyway, he wouldn't do it. Couldn't do it.

At least for the next few hours, he was blessedly

busy, and didn't have time to think about anything other than what he was doing. There'd been a pileup on the 405, and an odd strain of the flu, which caused appendicitis-like symptoms, so he was completely swamped, up to his eyes in puke and broken bones.

In the midst of the chaos, one of the nurses asked him to check a patient that wasn't his.

"She asked specifically for you," the nurse said with a shrug.

When he pulled back the curtain, he was shocked to find Emma there, the woman with cancer that he'd met at Faith's clinic. She was fast asleep, which gave him a moment to read the chart. She'd passed out in the grocery store.

"Emma?" Gently, he stroked her far-too-thin arm until her groggy eyes fluttered open. "Hey. What happened?"

She sighed. "I think it was just the pain."

"Have you been going to the acupressure appointments?"

"And massage therapy as well." Her eyes filled as she shook her head. "It's not enough. Faith told me to talk to you, that you'd get something stronger for the pain, but I thought I had it handled. Then the grocery store incident." She managed a smile but it was watery. "I guess the truth is, I'm getting scared."

This was the part he hated, not having all the answers, doing the best possible job and having it not be enough.

"Faith believes in you," she said. "So do I."

He looked into Emma's solemn eyes and inexplicably felt like crying. "We'll take care of you."

She sighed, even smiled, and trusting him, laid back and closed her eyes.

If only he trusted himself half as much.

Yeah, Faith believed in him. Enough to trust him with one of her patients. It was a stunning revelation, and a powerful one.

Soon, in one week, he'd go back to his life and Faith to hers. So simple in theory, but suddenly he didn't know how he could have ever believed it.

There was nothing simple about never seeing her again, never laughing with her, holding her, being with her. Nothing.

LATER, LUKE SAT ON A large rock on the beach outside his house and watched the waves hit. He'd conferred with Emma's specialist, and had learned what Faith had already told him weeks earlier—there was nothing to be done for her other than to make her comfortable.

He'd done that, while silently ranting at the fates that gave them such a vicious, demoralizing disease he couldn't conquer.

Luke liked to conquer his world, damn it, and hated it when something prevented him from doing so. And though they hadn't lost Emma yet, he felt the despair the same as if they had.

"What are you doing out here moping when I made you a Mexican casserole that tastes better than heaven?"

He looked up at Carmen as she lowered herself to the beach next to him. "Thanks, but I'm not really hungry."

She let out a theatrical, diva-like sigh. "You screw up with Faith?"

"No."

"Uh-huh. I suppose you messed up a good thing because you got to the usual two-month mark, and went claustrophobic. *Si?*"

"Actually, it's been nearly *three* months, and I never did get claustrophobic with Faith."

"Then she annoyed you in some way. Maybe she snores?"

"No."

"Okay, then, she chews with her mouth open. Or forgets to put the lid on the toothpaste."

"Carmen..." He scrubbed his hands over his face. "You're loco."

"*I'm* crazy? You're the one sitting here instead of being with your woman. You break up or something?"

"We're not together, and after next week when I'm done with the clinic, we're not seeing each other anymore."

"Well, who made up that brilliant rule?"

He sighed. "Don't you have a toilet to clean or something?"

"I'd rather bother you." She leaned back, made herself comfortable. "So let me get this straight...here's the first woman in forever to grab you by the heart strings and hold on tight, and you're going to walk away from her? And all this time I thought you were so smart."

"We both agreed this was just a temporary—" He broke off, stared at the pounding surf. Temporary. He was beginning to hate that word.

"A temporary sex thing?" She cackled. "Well, I'm all for that. Only it turned out to be more, you big, fancy idiot, and now what...you're too proud to say so?"

"More never works out for me. Not with my lifestyle."

"So a doctor isn't allowed to have a life now? You know what I think?"

"If I say yes, will you be quiet?"

"I think it's more than that. I think you're afraid."

He managed a laugh. "Don't be ridiculous."

"You're afraid to get married and have kids because

you think you'll be no better of a daddy than yours was."

Startled, he looked up at her. She nodded. "Your brother called me yesterday. Wanted to check up on you. I told him everything, so get over it. Matt said he thought maybe you didn't want to get involved since your parents didn't like the responsibility of having kids and never even looked at the two of you. He said that'd been his problem until he was knocked off his feet by some fancy, beautiful scientist he's going to marry."

He was going to kill his brother. "Carmen—"

"Right." She rose. "Mind my own business. Sure." She started to walk away, only to turn back. "I guess the thing I'm really surprised at is that Faith is being as stubborn and proud as you. I mean, we all know what's holding you back. Stupid, male pride. But what's holding her back? I would have thought at least one of you would have had the guts to fight for this." With that, she walked away.

The waves hit the shore with a relentless rhythm that now matched his new headache. He *did* know what held him back, and yes, maybe part of it was fear, part of it resignation that he could never have a normal family life, so he figured why try.

Sitting there on the sand watching Mother Nature

do her thing, he could admit, it'd always been easier to date casually, letting women in and out of his mental revolving door rather than try to solve the problem.

But what the hell held Faith back?

12

AND THEN IT WAS THEIR last weekend. Faith was going to open the clinic both days, as they were doing a special Women's Awareness Day on Sunday.

Luke had agreed to work the entire weekend, so readily that Faith actually let herself believe he didn't want it to end any more than she did.

Faith woke up feeling blue. She told herself she was worried about money, worried about a few patients, worried about a class she wanted to work into her schedule, worried about her blood sugar since late the night before. Driven by stress, she'd broken into Guy's personal stash of candy and had wolfed down two candy bars.

But what was really bothering her had nothing to do with any of those things and everything to do with the fact that tomorrow, after Women's Awareness Day, Luke would be gone.

Guy had bought some goodbye decorations at a party shop, and was dressing up their staff room. Shelby had made cookies, oatmeal with raisin, of course, and was proud of the fact that they contained no sugar or wheat.

They tasted like bricks, but that wasn't what caused the unswallowable lump in Faith's throat and she knew it.

Only two more days.

Forty-eight hours.

Two thousand eight hundred and eighty minutes.

She was mentally calculating the seconds when Luke walked into the room wearing his usual neat trousers and button-down shirt already shoved up to the elbows. He smiled at the decorations, grabbed a cookie and turned to Faith.

He took her breath.

Leaning back against the counter, he studied her while he took a bite. His eyes seemed to see everything, the way she'd pulled her wild hair back in an ineffective attempt to tame it. The crystals she'd put in her ears, guaranteed to make wishes come true...she'd be putting those to the test today. The high spots of color she could feel on her cheeks. The snug, unusually flattering knit dress she'd chosen hoping he'd notice that it actually made her look good—

His eyes flared with appreciation as they roamed over her, assuring her he'd noticed. He popped the rest of the cookie into his mouth and pushed away from the counter. "Those are awful," he said, and cupped her face. Tilting it up, he ran a thumb over her lower lip and destroyed a whole host of brain cells.

"That's because there's no sugar in them."

"Ah." Bending, he brushed his lips over hers. "Tonight, Faith?"

Her eyes drifted shut and she silently thanked him, because he'd made it so she couldn't think, which meant she could no longer calculate how much time she had left with him. "Tonight."

THAT NIGHT, LUKE HELPED her close up the clinic. "Dinner," he said, but she shook her head. She wasn't wasting a single moment of their second-to-last night together.

"Upstairs."

Slowly he nodded, and reaching out for her hand, led her up the stairs.

"Shower?" she murmured, dropping her coat right inside the front door and reaching for his. "Lots of steam and hot water?"

"If it involves a wet you."

They stripped each other on the way down the hall, between long, wet kisses and hands fighting for purchase. Faith opened his shirt and shoved it off his shoulders so she could touch the chest she could never get enough of. Luke unzipped her dress, nudged it to the floor and bending his dark head, put his mouth over her heart.

No. Too emotional, and if they went the emotional route tonight she was going to lose it. She wanted hot, hard, and fast, and with that in mind, she nibbled her way over his hard pec, scraping her teeth over his flat nipple.

He sucked in a harsh breath as his nipple beaded.

Looking up at him, she licked her way to his other side at the same time she shoved his pants down.

"Faith—" But he broke off with a choked breath and staggered back against the wall when she wrapped her fingers around his long, hard, hot length and stroked.

Luke actually saw stars, heard fireworks in his head. If he didn't slow her down, it was going to be over too soon, but then she stroked him again, slowly, with just the right pressure, and his toes started to curl. With a low oath, he reached for her but she held him off, dancing away, moving towards the bathroom.

He saw pink towels, and a pink toothbrush on the counter, with smiley faces on the handle. Then he caught her just as she turned on the water, caught her and spun her around, pressing her back against the cool glass door of the shower, sandwiching her there with his hot, hard body.

But she just smiled that smile that always melted him, and spun them again, holding *him* pinned against the door as she slowly, slowly, sank down to her knees in front of him.

"Faith—"

Her warm, silky mouth surrounded him and all the air left his lungs. Normally this was Luke's very favorite sexual act, and indeed his eyes were crossing as she kissed and caressed her way over him, but right now all he wanted was to be buried deep inside her warm, giving body. He wanted to look into her eyes, wanted to see she felt the same unbelievable, inexplicable pull, and he wanted, desperately, to pretend she could be his for more than just this last weekend. Wanted that so damn much he didn't know how to function.

But what she was doing to him... It took every ounce of control he had to pull her to her feet and into her bedroom, where he tossed the covers aside and gently tossed her onto the mattress.

"The shower—"

"Can wait." He kneeled on the bed. "I want you, Faith. I want you surrounding me, looking at me, seeing me...just me." Bending over her, he nuzzled at her throat. "Just me," he whispered, rubbing his jaw against the warm, full curve of her breast, watching the nipple harden even more, as if blindly seeking his mouth. His hand slid down her belly, between her thighs, and at the creamy wetness that slicked his fingers, he groaned.

"Oh, Luke..." Melting arms surrounded him. "I'm looking at you, seeing you, just you...just you, Luke." She opened her legs to accommodate him, and when he settled between them, she arched up, so that he could bury himself exactly where he wanted to be, deeply within her body. It was so powerful and complete his knees went weak, and he was grateful he hadn't tried to take her in the shower standing up or he'd have killed them both.

Pulling back, he thrust deep. She gasped and whimpered and sighed all at once, eyes closed, mouth open, body tight as an arrow beneath him. Her breasts were creamy and full, her nipples beaded and tight, her stomach quivering slightly as she waited impatiently, restlessly, for him to move again. When he didn't, when he could only hold on and stare down at her, overcome, she arched her hips, silently entreating him to take them both right off the edge of the cliff they clung to.

"Can't," he managed through gritted teeth. "Left the condom on the floor in the hallway in my pants."

With a soft moan, she sagged back. "Hurry."

He never moved so fast in his life, and when he sank into her again, suitably protected now, he combed his fingers into the hair at her temples and held her face, craving that connection as well. "Okay?"

"Yes—" she started, but the word turned into a moan when he pulled back, slick wet flesh dragging on slick wet flesh. Then he thrust deep and she pulled his face down and kissed him, long and deep as he moved within her, in a slow, even rhythm that built higher and higher until he could hardly breathe. Every part of him was alive, vibrantly alive, pushing him toward release far before he wanted to let go. Her face blurred, and he blinked furiously, wanting to keep that connection, needing to hear her, see her when she let go, when she lost herself in him. Higher and higher they went. His heart thundered, and an aching need for her singed his every nerve ending, until he felt himself start to slip off the edge of control. "I can't...Faith, I can't hold back...."

"Don't hold back, don't you dare—" Then her mouth opened in a surprised little O! as she arched against him as she began to shudder. It completely pulled him under, wave after wave of it, and all he could do was bury his face in her hair and let it take them both.

SUNDAY AFTERNOON OF Women's Awareness weekend came almost without warning. The decorations were still up, more cookies were out. Some of their regular patients had even left Luke gifts.

Faith walked around the staff room touching a balloon, stuffing the occasional—okay, not so occasional—cookie into her mouth, trying to remind herself this is what she'd wanted.

Luke had been awarded with a glowing report from his hospital in the morning paper. She read it with pride, knowing everything they'd said about him was true.

And more.

His job was secure, her clinic had never been in better shape. Things were great.

Pass the cookies.

He'd already walked right out of her life. Yes, he'd had some important staff meeting at the hospital, and yes, he'd apologized for having to run, and yes, he'd given her a kiss that had been at once perfection and soul-destroying, which hadn't helped at all.

"Faith? You going to be okay?"

Looking up she forced a smile at Shelby and Guy, both of whom were getting ready to leave. "Sure. Why wouldn't I be?"

They exchanged a long look between them that told her she had fooled exactly no one.

"It doesn't have to be over, you know."

Faith stared at Guy. "What? Of course it does. He's done here."

"But you're not done. Not with each other."

She let out a laugh that didn't deceive anyone any more than her smile had. "Oh, we're done. We agreed to be done."

Shelby sighed. "Oh, honey. For once, can't you think of yourself first? Can't you fight for something, if it means this much to you?"

"But the clinic—"

"Will be fine, even if you fall in love." Shelby smiled at her shocked expression. "The clinic will be fine, we'll be fine, and you'll be far more than fine if you let it happen. It's time, Faith. Time to do something for yourself instead of giving. Be selfish. Decide you want him for keeps and go after him."

"Do you need any helpful tips?" Guy asked sincerely. "Because I'd start with throwing out those old bunny slippers you wear."

"Oh, go on now," Faith said with a laugh, opening the door for them.

"Hey, come to dinner with us," Shelby said. "We're going for Japanese, at that new place that grills it up right in front of you."

"I'm not that hungry."

Now Shelby looked really worried. "Meet us

there," she whispered as she hugged Faith good-night. "If he doesn't show up soon."

Since she didn't trust her voice, Faith nodded and shut the door behind them, left alone with her far too numerous thoughts. If she closed her eyes, she could still feel Luke's last kiss. He'd held her face while their lips had clung in a moment at once both hot and so un-bearably sweet it brought a lump to her throat even now.

She was afraid it had been their last.

And when he didn't show up, she knew it had been.

LUKE TRIED TO LOOK interested in the meeting-that-wouldn't-end as he slowly cranked his wrist to glance at his watch—

"We boring you, Dr. Walker?"

This from Dr. Wesley Summerton, the president of the board of the hospital, the man who could make and break careers with one yawn, the man who'd just offered Luke an unprecedented second run as Depart-ment Head before his first run was even over.

"Of course not." He avoided Leo's knowing gaze. "It's just been long hours lately—"

"With the clinic, I know." Dr. Summerton nodded. "And I have to admit, you were an exceptionally good sport about the whole thing. Your staff seems happy, the media soaked you up, the clinic is doing a crackling business...it worked out, and we thank you wholeheartedly for it. But that's over now. You can call your free time your own again.''

Yes, he could. Only thing was, he didn't want his freedom. He wanted to be knocking on Faith's door, seeing if they really had nothing more to give each other.

Instead, here he was, being offered a position he'd wanted more than his next breath for so long, and all he could think about was Faith—her smile, her passion for life, her everything.

By the time he finally got out of the hospital, it was past midnight. Faith had been exhausted earlier, and pale. She needed her rest, she didn't need to be kept up all night by his hormones, no matter how badly he wanted her.

So with a heavy heart, and a damn erection, he turned towards home, wondering all the while if that was it. If it was already over.

Over before they'd really even begun.

WITHIN A FEW MINUTES of Shelby and Guy leaving for dinner, the violent spring storm that had been threatening all day finally hit. Perfect, as it suited Faith's mood. Thunder boomed, lightning flashed and rain thrashed against the windows of the clinic.

She tried to bury herself in paperwork, and it might have worked too, if her heart would just stop aching.

Or maybe that was her stomach.

Definitely, food would ease the problem, it always had before.

One more glance at her watch.

He wasn't coming back.

Well, fine. It was what she'd expected, what they'd agreed to, so time to get over herself. No better way to do that than having Japanese food.

Besides, she suddenly didn't want to be alone, couldn't stand her own company. So she drove to the restaurant in the booming thunder and driving rain and hoped Shelby and Guy had ordered a huge feast.

They were thrilled to see her, and greeted her with hugs that almost, *almost*, broke her. "You want to know how *I* get over a man I'm too chicken to fight for but really want?" Shelby asked, scooting over to make room for Faith.

Faith let out a choked laugh. "What are you talking about? You've never been too chicken to fight for a man."

Shelby cocked her head and considered. "You're right. Guy, you tell her then, tell her how to get over a man."

"Hey, I don't have to get over anyone either, they all have to get over me!"

Faith sighed, then jerked around at the sound of a startled cry at the table behind them.

A woman had pushed back from her table, her eyes wide, her mouth open, her hands on her obviously very pregnant belly. "Oh my God," she cried, and made the unmistakable face of a woman bearing down.

Her husband leaped up and whipped his head around uselessly, a panicked look on his face. "Uh...honey? A contraction?"

"Well, it's not a picnic!"

Faith tossed her cell phone to Guy to call an ambulance and kneeled at the woman's side. "Ma'am? You're in labor?"

"Oh God. Yes!"

Faith stroked her arm. "It's okay, it's going to be okay. My name is Faith and I'm a nurse."

"Oh, thank God." The woman gripped Faith's fingers so hard the bone crunched. "I have to push."

"I know, but not yet." Faith massaged the woman's hands and arms until she relaxed slightly. "Breathe."

"Oh my God, that helps. Keep doing it."

"I will, you keep breathing."

"I need drugs!"

"Okay, just relax a moment." She and Shelby had found that with certain pressure points and therapeutic massage, they could often ease a woman's birthing pain with no drugs at all, and she kept her hands on the woman. "What's your name?"

"Susan."

"Uh, honey?" Her husband bent down and let out a shaky smile. "Maybe we should go to the hospital?"

"Go away, Frank, you smell like teriyaki sauce and it's going to make me puke!"

Poor Frank retreated a few steps.

Susan's pulse was thready, she was sweaty and her breathing was uneven. "Take a nice deep breath," Faith reminded her. "There you go. Just breathe with me, okay?"

"Breathing doesn't work!"

"Humor me for a minute. In and out…there you go, that's right." Faith brushed the woman's hair back from her forehead and was encouraged at how her touch seemed to soothe her. "Now, how close are the contractions?"

"Uh-oh…her water broke," Shelby said from the woman's other side. "Guy?"

"Ambulance is on its way."

"Here comes another one!" Susan cried, and slid off her chair in a boneless heap to the floor, much to the horror of everyone dining around them.

The manager pushed his way through the crowd, a small Japanese man who was wringing his hands. "No baby here, no baby here! People eating!"

Guy intercepted him. "Do you have a private room where she can go until they arrive?"

"Yes, follow me." The Japanese man bowed to all the tables around them, apologizing.

Guy scooped up Susan, and with Faith holding her hand and Shelby leading the bewildered Frank, they followed the owner out of the main dining room. He took them into a room behind a beaded curtain. A huge papier-mâché dragon head peered down on them as they gently set down Susan on a pad.

She immediately started panting, and pulled her legs back as if to push. "I have to!" she cried when Faith tried to coax her into breathing again.

She was right, she had to, because when Faith checked, the baby was already crowning. The ambulance wasn't going to get here in time.

The baby came in less than four minutes.

The paramedics arrived in six.

Guy drove Frank to the hospital, Shelby went with Susan in the ambulance, and in all of the excitement, Faith ended up alone in the parking lot, in the pouring-down rain, realizing she was still starving.

In fact, her head was pounding, and her limbs felt a little shaky. She had that semi-queasy feeling she now recognized as low blood sugar but she didn't want to go back inside and eat alone. She could make it home.

Besides, she had to get used to being alone again.

She pulled out of the parking lot and was a little startled by how heavy the rain was, how slick the roads seemed. Dark had fallen, so she squinted through the windshield wipers that were furiously working to keep her vision clear.

Slow and easy, she told herself, and was thankful for the light traffic. Up ahead the light switched from red to green and she kept her foot on the accelerator. Then, unexpectedly, it turned red again. When she hit the brake, the car went into a slide, and her heart kicked up into her throat.

She passed through the crosswalk. Skidded, skidded...and finally stopped just over the line.

Gasping, she sagged back. She was okay.

Except she hadn't realized how badly her head hurt, or how shaky she really was. The lack of dinner combined with the candy bars from the night before really had gotten to her. She should have taken a sugar pill, which she kept with her in her purse for her low-sugar days. If she could pop one in her mouth now, within a minute she'd feel better, good enough to get home and feed herself. And if she managed that without killing herself on the road, she promised herself right there and then, in a solemn vow, she'd never, ever, screw up her diet again. Reaching for the passenger seat and her purse—

It wasn't there. She'd left her purse at the restaurant.

The light turned green, and she decided she was closer to home, that she'd call the restaurant when she got there to tell them she'd left her purse, and again hit the gas. The rain continued to hit the car hard, bouncing up off the trunk, so that she could hardly hear herself think. The swish, swish of the windshield wipers added to the mix, joining the pounding in her head.

God, she was so very tired, but finally, *finally*, she pulled onto her street. She waited for the overwhelming relief, she was almost there, safe and sound no less, but it was all she could do to get the car into the driveway.

Shaking like a leaf, she turned off the engine—and put her forehead to the steering wheel. She just felt so...damn...tired....

13

LUKE DROVE HOME FROM his late meeting on autopilot. In his driveway, engine still running, windshield wipers whisking away the drumming rain as fast as it hit the window, he stared out into the night at his house.

It was dark. Probably cold.

No doubt Carmen had the entire place clean as a whistle, but the warm, sweet touches of a real home wouldn't be there. They never had been. There were no flowers on the table, freshly picked from the yard, with specific scents for specific needs. There was no fresh tea brewing that would act as a soother, an antibiotic or a mood lifter. There would be no pink toothbrush with a smiley face on the handle sitting on the bathroom counter next to a wide and baffling array of pots and bottles, all of which would smell like Faith.

Mesmerized by the movement from the windshield wipers and the headlights reflecting off the windows of the front of his house, all of which were dark with no life behind them, he let out a long sigh.

He felt...strange. As if he was searching for something in his life, something just out of reach. He couldn't go on without this...this thing, and he couldn't quite figure out what it was.

No, wait. That wasn't true. It wasn't a thing he was missing, but a person. A small, curvy, beautiful red-headed person nearly as stubborn as himself, and that was quite a feat, as he was pretty damn stubborn.

Faith.

With her name on his lips, he suddenly knew what it was. He'd fallen in love with her. And damn it, instead of facing that, instead of telling her, he'd tried to ignore it, tried to let it pass. After all, he had work, he had a meeting, he had...nothing, absolutely nothing as important as this.

Since when did he take the easy way out? Never. And he wasn't going to now either. Shoving the car in reverse, he craned his neck around and maneuvered himself out of the driveway and back into the dark, stormy night.

This wouldn't—couldn't—wait, and though it was nearly one in the morning, and the roads were a mess, he drove toward Faith's house. Not wanting to scare her with a knock this late, he grabbed his cell phone to call ahead and warn her. He was coming over, and they were going to face this.

But unbelievably, she didn't answer. He stared down at his cell phone, but he'd dialed correctly.

So...where was she? Had someone come to the

clinic late, needing assistance? Yeah, that was probably it, and he sped up a little, hating the thought of her alone in that place with someone she didn't know. She thought she was invincible, that since all she wanted to do was help people, no one would hurt her.

Unsettled, he pulled into the driveway, right behind her car. Her headlights were still on, and so were the windshield wipers, which had him all the more worried. Her car was stilling running and it'd been parked at an odd angle, as if she'd been so exhausted—

Then he saw the dark figure slumped over the wheel and his heart jerked to a halt. Racing through the rain, he whipped open her car door. "Faith," he said hoarsely, and hunkered beside her, ignoring the rain deluging him, running down his face, soaking into his clothes. With one hand on her body, which was warm enough at least, he pulled out his cell phone and dialed 9-1-1 for an ambulance.

She lifted her head, and through her streaming hair, blinked at him. "Luke?"

"Just me." He finished with dispatch, pocketed the phone and took a deep breath to steady himself. He was a doctor, a damned good one, so there was no logical reason for all his medical training to fly out the window simply because the woman he'd fallen in love with was in her car in a semiconscious state, confused, and looking like death warmed over. "You passed out, do you remember?"

She closed her eyes and put a hand to her head. "I'm fine now, if you'll just move, I could get out."

Right. And she'd crumple to the ground. "You're slurring your words," he said as calmly as he could. "You've bottomed out, haven't you."

"What?"

"Your blood sugar."

"No...I..." She set her head back against the head-rest and kept her eyes closed. "Maybe."

With every four-letter word in the book running through his head, he put his fingers over the pulse at her wrist. Thready. Her skin was clammy, and beneath his fingers he could feel her trembling. Damn it. "Where the hell is your purse?"

"I left it in the restaurant by accident."

He shoved his hand in his pocket and pulled out his Tic Tacs. Not exactly a sugar pill, but better than nothing. Shaking two into his hand, he held them up to her mouth.

Her tongue touched the palm of his hand and he felt the most irresponsible, inappropriate surge of lust, which added to his anger. "You didn't eat dinner?"

"I—"

"You ignored all the signs and just kept going? Is that it?"

"Well—"

"What, you think you're the Energizer Bunny? Christ, Faith, you have to listen to your body."

"I know, I—"

"Be quiet." He carried her to the door of the clinic, wanting her inside until the ambulance came, so mad *he* was now shaking.

"The keys are still in the car," she said when they were both looking at the front door.

He set her down, ran to get the keys, then raced back. He might have lit into her again, but she was leaning against the door looking tired and dejected and so pathetic he didn't have the heart for it.

Besides, he'd come for another reason entirely, and looking at her now, into her eyes that she thought hid so much and yet showed him everything, he melted all over again. "Faith..."

"Could you unlock the door?" she asked quietly. "And then I swear, I'll go in and eat. I've already had my epiphany, Luke, so you don't need to waste your night yelling at me. I promised myself in that car I would never, ever, let my blood sugar get so low again, that I would eat far more regularly, that my health has to come first."

He unlocked the door and she moved inside, then turned to face him with a wan smile. "Thank you."

And then, unbelievably, she started to shut the door. In his face.

"Faith."

Her eyes met his, reluctantly, he thought. His own fault. "Aren't you in the least bit curious as to why I'm here at one in the morning?"

Her eyes widened. "It's that late?"

He put his foot in the door in case she decided she didn't want to hear this and tried to shut it. She was a healer, she wouldn't want to break his foot. "I had a reason for coming here."

"You mean before you started yelling at me?" With a little moan, she held her head. "Damn it."

"Sit down before you fall down," he demanded, terrified all over again. He pushed her into a chair. Charged to the staff refrigerator and pulled out juice and some sliced cheese. He shoved them at her, not relaxing until she bit into the cheese. He could hear the siren of the ambulance now, and Faith let out a frustrated sound so devoid of any real temper he got even more unnerved. "You're going to the hospital."

"I'm not going anywhere," she said. "I'll be fine once I've eaten and—"

"You're going and I'm going to run the tests myself."

"I'm not going, Luke." Her eyes were still closed, and she still hadn't moved a muscle.

He lifted her into his arms.

"I'm feeling fine now...Luke—"

"You didn't give your body rest, you didn't eat right."

"Yes, but I—"

"You work in a self-healing clinic, and you don't even use the techniques on yourself?"

"I told you, I—"

"Yes, tell me. What the hell is that about?"

"Well, you're a fine one to talk!" Feeling much better from the candy he'd given her, even if it was only a temporary fix, Faith poked him in the chest with a finger. "You work shifts just as long as I do, you ignore all of your own needs for your patients, you—"

"If I had a disease to take care of, I promise you, I sure as hell would!"

"Really? Well..."

"Well, what?" Luke demanded, nose to nose with her. Thunder boomed and neither of them jumped. "You don't have anything to say, do you?"

"I do so, I—" She frowned.

"Oh, *now* you're going to be quiet?"

She crossed her arms, the picture of an irritated woman. "I'm done yelling at you—this is stupid."

"Really?" He put his wet nose to hers. "Try this for stupid. I came here to tell you something, something rather important actually, and I find you slumped over the wheel looking like death warmed over. You scared the hell out of me, damn it."

"I didn't mean to, but God, Luke, you're just so bossy."

"Bossy?" He nearly choked over the word.

"And then I thought I was never going to see you again, and—"

"Wait a minute. Back the damn train up. You were the one who said you didn't want this to continue after my three months—"

"And do you think I don't know that?"

His head was spinning, spinning away, she drove him that crazy.

"Luke, damn it, I—"

"Love you," they both shouted at the same time. Then blinked. Stared at each other.

Lightning flashed.

The ambulance pulled up. Two medics hopped out and peered into the clinic. Both of them recognized Luke, who held up a hand, signaling they needed a moment.

"What?" Luke asked her hoarsely, stepping close. "What did you just say?"

"The same thing as you, I think." Very carefully, very purposely, Faith set her head down on his chest. She needed the support. Taking a peek, she saw Luke's eyes, which had been dark with fear and anger and a whole host of things only a moment ago, were now wide with shock.

Much, she imagined, the way hers were.

He loved her. Was it really possible?

As if he was the weak one now, he stumbled back, and tugging her with him, sat down hard on a chair.

Faith landed in his lap.

The medics started forward, but Luke glared at them until they both retreated back a few steps. "Faith?"

"Yes?"

"Let's try that again, but you go first this time."

"Oh no," she said demurely, her heart light for the first time in weeks. *Months.* Since the first time he'd walked through her door, as a matter of fact. "You came out in the middle of the night to talk to me. The least I can do is let you go first."

His hair was slicked close to his head, and he blinked rainwater out of his eyes as he stared down at her. "You're messing with my head, right?"

She was, and upon closer inspection of his fierce expression, she nearly melted, for he had stark fear lingering behind his eyes, fear she'd put there. "I'm sorry I drive you so crazy, Luke. I promise I'll never take risks with my health again if you promise to give us everything you give your patients."

"I didn't know you wanted me to give *us* anything," he said very quietly.

"I know, and that's partly my fault, too, because I didn't tell you how I feel."

"But you're going to tell me now."

"Yes." She smiled through her sudden tears and cupped his face. "I love you, Dr. Luke Walker. I love you with all my heart."

"Even if I'm...bossy?"

"Especially because you're bossy. That's my favorite part of you, your utter confidence, your knowledge that you're always right—"

He shut her up with a kiss that went a long way toward warming up her chilled body.

"Uh, Dr. Walker?" One of the medics once again stepped forward. "Is someone going to the hospital?" He wrapped his arms around himself. "Because it's damn wet out there, and—"

"No one is going to the hospital," Faith said, her eyes on Luke, who lifted a brow.

"Did you say *I* was the bossy one?" he asked.

"Yes. And don't think it's escaped my notice that I've done all the talking."

"Yeah." He didn't break eye contact with her. "Sorry, guys, false alarm. Have the hospital bill me for the run, but I think I've got this situation under control."

He waited until they'd driven off into the night before he spoke. "I thought my life was complete, even though my brother and Carmen kept telling me I was wrong, and that I needed love."

"That must have gone over well."

"I wasn't looking for this," he said quietly. "Wasn't looking for anything but what I had at work, and yet it's the oddest thing..." He stroked a wet strand of hair off her cheek but left his fingers on her skin. "I can't imagine my life the way it was before you."

"That's incredibly sweet," she whispered, snuggling even closer. "And I'll want to hear that again and again, but right now I'm just looking for a review of those three little words that begins with 'I' and ends with 'you' and has a big word in the middle that starts with 'L'."

"I'm getting there," he said, undeterred and apparently not willing to be rushed.

She wriggled a little on his lap, just a little, until his arms tightened and his breath caught.

"Okay, now you're trying to rush me," he accused, holding her hips to keep her still. "I'm trying to give you my heart here and you're thinking of sex."

"I'm thinking of sex, yes, but also more. I want your heart, Luke, more than anything. I promise to be careful with it."

"Yeah. Careful would be good, as I've never given it

away before." He let out a slow breath. "I love you, Faith, and I think I have since I first laid eyes on you."

Joy sang through her and she wrapped her arms around him. "Do you think we can go upstairs now?"

Grinning, he surged up with her in his arms. "I was just afraid you and your hot little bod would distract me and I wouldn't say what I'd come to say."

"Well..." She bit his lower lip, then soothed it with a lick of her tongue. "You've said what you wanted to say now, right? So...you're ready for a distraction?"

"Definitely, though you should know our first activity is going to be to eat. But distract away."

"Distracting away." Leaning in, she whispered a naughty suggestion, something that would keep them busy until sunrise.

His eyes darkened. "Sounds good, but I'm thinking beyond sunrise."

"Okay...how about until...tomorrow night?"

"Nope."

God. She pulled back, horrified. She'd assumed he'd meant there were no more time restrictions on them, but he'd never really said—

"I'm thinking forever," he said. "Does forever work for you? Sharing my life, heart and soul forever?"

She swallowed hard past the lump in her throat and nodded past her tears. "Well, I suppose it's only fair," she whispered. "Since that's how long I want to share mine with you."

____Epilogue____

Two weeks later

FAITH SAT IN THE STAFF room, a cup of green tea in front of her, fascinated by her own left hand.

"Would you stop it?" Shelby complained. "You're blinding me."

Faith grinned as she, for the hundredth time, shifted her fingers to catch the light on her diamond engagement ring.

"Hey, slackers," Luke said as he came into the room, dressed to see patients. "It's Saturday and you have a full clinic." He clapped his hands like the dictator he sometimes forgot he wasn't. "Let's hit it."

Then he caught sight of what Faith was drinking and went utterly still. "What are you doing?"

"Drinking green tea. Did you know it has qualities that help regulate blood sugar and insulin levels?"

"It also lowers cholesterol," Shelby said helpfully.

Luke took the cup away.

"Hey," Faith protested. "I just made that."

He set it on the counter and turned back to her. "Green tea isn't good for pregnant women."

Shelby gasped.

So did Faith. "First of all," she said slowly. "How do you even know that?"

"Hey, you're not the only one who knows some naturopathic stuff."

Faith smiled, but it slowly faded. "I'm not pregnant, Luke."

"I thought we weren't sure."

She sighed. "I am today." She didn't look at him for a moment because suddenly she felt...uncertain. How would he feel about that? Relieved? Upset?

But then he was right there, gently lifting her chin, kissing her softly. "Are you okay?"

"For now," she answered as honestly as she could. "But I have to admit to an odd disappointment."

"Yeah." His eyes were soft on hers. "I know."

"I still want to wear your ring," she said, possessively pulling it to her chest.

"God, I hope so," he said fervently.

Faith stood up to hug him. "And there's always..." She leaned and bit his earlobe.

Shelby rolled her eyes. "Take it to a bedroom."

"Always...what?" Luke asked huskily.

Faith soothed the nip she'd just taken with her tongue. "Practicing," she whispered.

"I'm not hearing this," Shelby said, putting her hands to her ears.

Luke's hands slid down Faith's body and his mouth nibbled at her throat. "Practicing...I like that. I like that a lot."

Is your man too good to be true?

Hot, gorgeous AND romantic?
If so, he could be a Harlequin® Blaze™ series cover model!

Our grand-prize winners will receive a trip for two to New York City to shoot the cover of a Blaze novel, and will stay at the luxurious Plaza Hotel.

Plus, they'll receive $500 U.S. spending money!

The runner-up winners will receive $200 U.S. to spend on a romantic dinner for two.

It's easy to enter!

In 100 words or less, tell us what makes your boyfriend or spouse a true romantic and the perfect candidate for the cover of a Blaze novel, and include in your submission two photos of this potential cover model.

All entries must include the written submission of the contest entrant, two photographs of the model candidate and the Official Entry Form and Publicity Release forms completed in full and signed by both the model candidate and the contest entrant. Harlequin, along with the experts at Elite Model Management, will select a winner.

For photo and complete Contest details, please refer to the Official Rules on the next page. All entries will become the property of Harlequin Enterprises Ltd. and are not returnable.

Please visit www.blazecovermodel.com to download a copy of the Official Entry Form and Publicity Release Form or send a request to one of the addresses below.

Please mail your entry to: **Harlequin Blaze Cover Model Search**

In U.S.A.	In Canada
P.O. Box 9069	P.O. Box 637
Buffalo, NY	Fort Erie, ON
14269-9069	L2A 5X3

No purchase necessary. Contest open to Canadian and U.S. residents who are 18 and over. Void where prohibited. Contest closes September 30, 2003.

HBCVRMODEL1

HARLEQUIN BLAZE COVER MODEL SEARCH CONTEST 3569 OFFICIAL RULES
NO PURCHASE NECESSARY TO ENTER

1. To enter, submit two (2) 4" x 6" photographs of a boyfriend or spouse (who must be 18 years of age or older) taken no later than three (3) months from the time of entry: a close-up, waist up, shirtless photograph; and a fully clothed full-length photograph, then, tell us, in 100 words or fewer, why he should be a Harlequin Blaze cover model and how he is romantic. Your complete "entry" must include: (i) your essay, (ii) the Official Entry Form and Publicity Release Form printed below completed and signed by you (as "Entrant"), (iii) the photographs (with your hand-written name, address and phone number, and your model's name, address and phone number on the back of each photograph), and (iv) the Publicity Release Form and Photograph Representation Form printed below completed and signed by your model (as "Model"), and should be sent via first-class mail to either: Harlequin Blaze Cover Model Search Contest 3569, P.O. Box 9069, Buffalo, NY, 14269-9069, or Harlequin Blaze Cover Model Search Contest 3569, P.O. Box 637, Fort Erie, Ontario L2A 5X3. All submissions must be in English and be received no later than September 30, 2003. Limit: one entry per person, household or organization. **Purchase or acceptance of a product offer does not improve your chances of winning.** All entry requirements must be strictly adhered to for eligibility and to ensure fairness among entries.

2. Ten (10) Finalist submissions (photographs and essays) will be selected by a panel of judges consisting of members of the Harlequin editorial, marketing and public relations staff, as well as a representative from Elite Model Management (Toronto) Inc., based on the following criteria:

Aptness/Appropriateness of submitted photographs for a Harlequin Blaze cover—70%
Originality of Essay—20%
Sincerity of Essay—10%

In the event of a tie, duplicate finalists will be selected. The photographs submitted by finalists will be posted on the Harlequin website no later than November 15, 2003 (at www.blazecovermodel.com), and viewers may vote, in rank order, on their favorite(s) to assist in the panel of judges' final determination of the Grand Prize and Runner-up winning entries based on the above judging criteria. All decisions of the judges are final.

3. All entries become the property of Harlequin Enterprises Ltd. and none will be returned. Any entry may be used for future promotional purposes. Elite Model Management (Toronto) Inc. and/or its partners, subsidiaries and affiliates operating as "Elite Model Management" will have access to all entries including all personal information, and may contact any Entrant and/or Model in its sole discretion for their own business purposes. Harlequin and Elite Model Management (Toronto) Inc. are separate entities with no legal association or partnership whatsoever having no power to bind or obligate the other or create any expressed or implied obligation or responsibility on behalf of the other, such that Harlequin shall not be responsible in any way for any acts or omissions of Elite Model Management (Toronto) Inc. or its partners, subsidiaries and affiliates in connection with the Contest or otherwise and Elite Model Management shall not be responsible in any way for any acts or omissions of Harlequin or its partners, subsidiaries and affiliates in connection with the contest or otherwise.

4. All Entrants and Models must be residents of the U.S. or Canada, be 18 years of age or older, and have no prior criminal convictions. The contest is not open to any Model that is a professional model and/or actor in any capacity at the time of the entry. Contest void wherever prohibited by law; all applicable laws and regulations apply. Any litigation within the Province of Quebec regarding the conduct or organization of a publicity contest may be submitted to the Régie des alcools, des courses et des jeux for a ruling, and any litigation regarding the awarding of a prize may be submitted to the Régie only for the purpose of helping the parties reach a settlement. Employees and immediate family members of Harlequin Enterprises Ltd., D.L. Blair, Inc., Elite Model Management (Toronto) Inc. and their parents, affiliates, subsidiaries and all other agencies, entities and persons connected with the use, marketing or conduct of this Contest are not eligible to enter. Acceptance of any prize offered constitutes permission to use Entrants' and Models' names, essay submissions, photographs or other likenesses for the purposes of advertising, trade, publication and promotion on behalf of Harlequin Enterprises Ltd., its parent, affiliates, subsidiaries, assigns and other authorized entities involved in the judging and promotion of the contest without further compensation to any Entrant or Model, unless prohibited by law.

5. Finalists will be determined no later than October 30, 2003. Prize Winners will be determined no later than January 31, 2004. Grand Prize Winners (consisting of winning Entrant and Model) will be required to sign and return Affidavit of Eligibility/Release of Liability and Model Release forms within thirty (30) days of notification. Non-compliance with this requirement and within the specified time period will result in disqualification and an alternate will be selected. Any prize notification returned as undeliverable will result in the awarding of the prize to an alternate set of winners. All travelers (or parent/legal guardian of a minor) must execute the Affidavit of Eligibility/Release of Liability prior to ticketing and must possess required travel documents (e.g. valid photo ID) where applicable. Travel dates specified by Sponsor but no later than May 30, 2004.

6. Prizes: One (1) Grand Prize—the opportunity for the Model to appear on the cover of a paperback book from the Harlequin Blaze series, and a 3 day/2 night trip for two (Entrant and Model) to New York, NY for the photo shoot of Model which includes round-trip coach air transportation from the commercial airport nearest the winning Entrant's home to New York, NY, (or, in lieu of air transportation, $100 cash payable to Entrant and Model, if the winning Entrant's home is within 250 miles of New York, NY), hotel accommodations (double occupancy) at the Plaza Hotel and $500 cash spending money payable to Entrant and Model, (approximate prize value: $8,000), and one (1) Runner-up Prize of $200 cash payable to Entrant and Model for a romantic dinner for two (approximate prize value: $200). Prizes are valued in U.S. currency. Prizes consist of only those items listed as part of the prize. No substitution of prize(s) permitted by winners. All prizes are awarded jointly to the Entrant and Model of the winning entries, and are not severable - prizes and obligations may not be assigned or transferred. Any change to the Entrant and/or Model of the winning entries will result in disqualification and an alternate will be selected. Taxes on prize are the sole responsibility of winners. Any and all expenses and/or items not specifically described as part of the prize are the sole responsibility of winners. Harlequin Enterprises Ltd. and D.L. Blair, Inc., their parents, affiliates, and subsidiaries are not responsible for errors in printing of Contest entries and/or game pieces. No responsibility is assumed for lost, stolen, late, illegible, incomplete, inaccurate, non-delivered, postage due or misdirected mail or entries. In the event of printing or other errors which may result in unintended prize values or duplication of prizes, all affected game pieces or entries shall be null and void.

7. Winners will be notified by mail. For winners' list (available after March 31, 2004), send a self-addressed, stamped envelope to: Harlequin Blaze Cover Model Search Contest 3569 Winners, P.O. Box 4200, Blair, NE 68009-4200, or refer to the Harlequin website (at www.blazecovermodel.com).

Contest sponsored by Harlequin Enterprises Ltd., P.O. Box 9042, Buffalo, NY 14269-9042.

HBCVRMODEL2

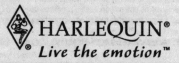

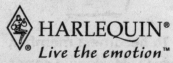